for Jendalyn

THIS IS WHAT YOU GET

BY

ANTHONY DRAGONETTI

FERAL DOVE BOOKS

MAINE, USA

2024

Inside the house is fine. No one else can see it. I can see it. That bothers me. What I think doesn't matter, though. I have to live with it. It's other people I'm worried about.

Outside the house is not fine. I can live with my self-judgment. It's the looks that linger a little too long that hurt. I make it hurt. I've got bite marks on all my knuckles. Some of them are scabbed. I can't help it. I get embarrassed and I bite down before I can think about it.

Sometimes I la-la-la out loud to myself so I can't hear the little voice narrating every embarrassment I've ever suffered. How much am I expected to take? A person has limits. I'm not special.

The la-la-las started making me even more self-conscious, so I trained myself to stop doing them. Sometimes I slip up and one gets out. I try very hard.

You're such a stupid asshole. You idiot. You don't try. You've never tried in your life. If something isn't handed to you with no effort on your part, it's the apocalypse.

I'm bleeding. The pain in my hand does a better job of distracting me anyway. I walk into the park and turn up the music in my headphones. Metallic racket to drown out what people say. I don't want to hear it. They look at me and make little asides to their companions. I'm not a prop for your routine. The jokes aren't funny. I haven't heard any, but I can tell.

The first lap begins. Every day it's the same path, taking the same forks, entering and exiting from the same gates. Sometimes they do work with these trucks. Hoses running everywhere. It blocks the paths. And then there are the kids from the school down the block getting marched around for whatever reason. Impossible to get around them. It makes me so mad. My teeth grind thinking about it.

I'm conscious of my breathing and how my limbs look while I move. I tuck my arms in closer, opening and closing my hands. Over by where the bathrooms are, I see a woman looking at me. It's for less than a second, and she averts her eyes. It doesn't mean anything. I'm almost done with my lap.

She's onto you. She knows all about you. She's going to tell her friends about it later and they're all going to laugh at you.

I saw this guy in the park, she'll say. There was definitely something wrong with him. And then I caught him looking at me. I thought I was going to have to hide in a toilet.

The thought of it makes me want to throw up. My nails are digging into my palms. La-la-la. I'm telling myself it doesn't matter, but I don't believe it. I have to know what she saw. I need to defend myself. I am not fodder for your big night out. I round a corner but stay close enough to see which way she goes. She's heading for the exit I don't usually take. I feel a strain, but I have to do this. Everyone in the park knows what I'm about to do. They're pretending to hold conversations while they keep one eye on me.

Discreet, I think. I am now going to be discreet.

I follow her from a distance out of the park. The streets aren't too crowded. I catch some glances here and there, but I'm so focused on her that they don't bother me. I know she won't see me. I can't let her. She'll recognize me. The man with that face and stuttering gait. Walking like a freak. I move fast. This goes on for blocks. The sidewalks empty out as we move off the main avenues. Residential streets with one or two people passing.

I fall back more, hoping it makes me less noticeable. People have a right to walk around their neighborhood. How many people even live around here? Half a million? Mind your business. But she turns her head, and I feel my stomach try to escape out of my throat. La-la-la. She keeps walking. She didn't notice me. Oh my God. I think my heart is going to stop.

She's making her way up the stairs to the entrance of her apartment building. I speed up as she unlocks the door, trying to get in behind her.

I just moved in, sorry. We haven't met. Yeah, I'm on the third floor.

That sounds good. I'll say that. Except I'm not quick enough, and she's inside before I can reach the top of the stairs. I watch her turn down the hall from the other side of the glass. I give the knob a defeated jiggle, but it opens. The luck of a cheap landlord. I step down the hallway I watched her enter and there she is, putting the key in her door. For the first time, she sees me and jolts. She recognizes me. I know it.

I   approach   her   anyway.

Hey, I'm sorry. I just moved in. Can I ask you something about the laundry room?

She's not buying it. She knows I'm the man from the park. Her keys drop out of her hand and jingle against the ground, like a horror movie.

Okay, I'm sorry. I'm sorry. I don't live here. Please just talk to me for a second.

Her eyes widen as she fumbles for the keys, trying to pick out the right one again.

I'm not going to hurt you. Please. Do I look like I'd hurt anyone? I just need to ask you something.

She looks like she's about to scream, but I have to get the question out.

What did you see back there? In the park. What do you see right now? Help me understand. What do you see when you look at me?

5   The most important part for them is making sure that it appears what they are doing to me is out of kindness. Whether it is or not isn't important. As long as their conscience is clear and it looks like they're doing all they can to the outside world, then this is the arrangement.

Being sent to my room at my age. If I knew it all would have turned out this way.

Enough. I'm not starting that again. I'm alive. I have a place to live. Not everyone can say that. I don't starve. My needs are mostly accounted for. Not everyone can say that. Yes, those are the lines. That's what I'm supposed to think when I start getting agitated. That's what Mother tells me. Then I get told to go sit in the room until I can compose myself. I am asked to compose myself several times a day.

I'm a good son, of course. I don't want to make them feel uncomfortable or worse. I know it makes them afraid. That's why I sit here when told. The doctor, who I don't believe is a doctor, says I need a healthy outlet.

Exercise was the first idea. That didn't go well. Mother always said I'm smart and imaginative. The doctor agrees I'm smart and imaginative. Maybe I can do something with that.

My hands don't do what I tell them to. It's embarrassing. The doctor suggested painting and I tried to explain my condition, but he said it's not real. It's a symptom of what we've been discussing. I'm making it up, in nicer words. My powerful imagination. Why not use it for something therapeutic?

OK, I'll imagine something therapeutic.

Hello, Bobby. I pull you from nothing and give you life because I hate you. I hate the name Bobby, so that's what I call you. If I can think about you without getting angry, then this won't work.

Who are you? I know what you are, but who? Are you a sensitive little boy? Yes, but certainly not a baby. I had to go through being born, but imagining all that for you doesn't serve my purpose. My birth was unremarkable. I didn't come out blue. No umbilical cord strangling me. No mark upon me to suggest an evil presence. I gestated until I was quite heavy. My poor little mother. Nothing happened. They smacked me, I took a breath, and then I was handed off. In a few days I was taken home in the back of a recently purchased used sedan.

I didn't cry. So, I'm told. I was a good, quiet boy. A lump that just wanted to eat and move as little as possible. So, I'm told. The story goes I never crawled. I simply stood up and walked one day. I have my doubts. Mothers have a way of portraying their boys as being able to walk on water and it causes problems later. My poor mother.

Poor me.

For once.

Ever?

Yes, eventually.

But not yet.

What should I make you look like Bobby? Giving you a name isn't enough. I need to give people something to sink their teeth into. I think I want them to feel sorry for you, but not too sorry that they'll avoid watching you suffer. The suffering is where that emotional hook comes from. If things went well for you, no one would care. And if you're beautiful? They'll want to hurt you themselves. But they're cowards so they'd rather be voyeurs.

Fast forward to when things happen. I think you're twelve years old, Bobby. Your body is starting to change. There will be ramifications later. But it's starting. It's noticeable to anyone looking for it. Worst of all, it's all you can think about. No one has explained what these changes mean to you. What they mean for boys.

A series of questions, a series of rooms. All of these people coming and going throughout your life cutting a piece of you off along the way. One would assume it all leads to some meaning. There must be a point where a step back would reveal the necessity of suffering. The logic reveals itself.

This is a harmful belief that should be forgotten. It has only ever led to more trouble.

One lesson that should be learned here is that there is no story. Not only here. Out there, too.

Well, this happened to me. Therefore, this happened and so I am like this. A leads to B leads to C. Even better if there is some perceived obstacle for me, the hero, to overcome. Call it tough love, but you need to get it through your head that these neat, tidy stories aren't real.

Bobby, this is just how it is for you. A device close enough to the real thing to be believable. I have a point to make. I need to make everyone understand how bad it is here.

A man sits on the edge of the bed with a woman he met an hour ago. He's looking at her sheets and silently declaring yet another successful night out. She's finishing her shower. She insisted when they got there that she absolutely needed a shower before anything. He pretended to protest but he was relieved she said so. Body odor repulses him. The sight of flesh up close does also, but luckily most people prefer it in the dark.

The bathroom door opens and he turns to look at her with his practiced grin already in place. She stands in the doorway in an exaggerated pose, one hand barely keeping the robe closed around her body. He focuses on how her neckline looks and can't help but remember. It comes back to him all at once like a movie that's taken over his vision:

The ball sails over the boy's head. Hot panic flushes his face as he watches its trajectory. It bounces off the door they all knew it would hit. No one moves.

Car!

They scatter to the closest sidewalks, hoping no one is home. It's their only ball. Someone has to get it if they want to keep playing.

You missed it, you go get it!

The boy attempts to protest, but he can't come up with a good reason why he shouldn't go. The ball sits against the concrete lip separating the small, dead vegetable garden from the walkway to the door.

Get it! Get it!

He tells them to keep quiet and walks on useless tiptoes toward the brownstone. Each footfall on the asphalt somehow pounds as loud as his heart. His fingers reach the ball when the door opens and a woman who looks his mother's age smiles at him.

You young men aren't up to any trouble, are you?

He is old enough to intuit, though unable to articulate, how charged that question is. He doesn't want to shake his head no. He wants to say yes. Yes, I am up to trouble. The words won't come. He looks her up and down, focusing on how close her robe is to opening if she loosens her grip around its middle. The way her skin is shining in the sun because of her sweat.

He remembers his parents had pointed her out one time while they were walking to the supermarket. His mother would say to stay away from her and people like her. The boy didn't understand what that meant. What about her?

Some people, his mother began then paused to search for the right words, are a little different from you and I. They're touched.

Touched?

She's fucking crazy, his father said with satisfaction. Why else would she be walking around half-naked in the winter doing that stuff with her eyes?

His mother made a face and repeated to the boy to just stay away. His father had completely turned his head to watch the woman walk, not even pretending to hide it, and turned back around to give his son a look like he wanted to tell him something telepathically.

Yeah, his father said, you don't want any of that. You wouldn't know what to do with it.

His mother shot a look at his father. He knows it means nothing. The boy knows it means nothing.

Now here she was, right in front of him.

His peach fuzz has been darkening by the day. He's become prone to cultivating a particular smell that makes his mother turn her nose up and call him a disgusting animal. There's also the increasing number of instances where he hasn't been able to stand up whenever he wants. The universal shame boys experience when their bodies start to know what they want before their brains do.

Would you like to come inside?

He knows that he should refuse. It would be easy to say no. His entire being is screaming yes. Yes, I would like to come inside. Yes, I am looking for trouble. Yes.

Would you like to come inside, she says again.

Yes, almost escapes his lips too quickly, too eagerly.

What for, he says.

Would you like to see some pictures? I think you'll like them. It'll be fun.

He gets lightheaded for the first time in that mind exploding way. Every other time will feel like an imitation in comparison. She's already slipping back in, and he follows her without speaking.

The hallway is dark, but not dark enough to hide the filthy carpet covering the floor and steps. She leads him to the last apartment on the first floor and opens the door to an even darker kitchen. The only light is in the back parlor. She looks behind to make sure he's following and guides him towards a small sofa.

Make yourself comfortable. I'm going to get those pictures. Do you want anything to drink?

What do you have?

Water.

He thinks he'll throw up anything he swallows so he shakes his head no. She disappears into another one of the dark rooms, leaving him looking at his feet. Another first for him is this view of the chasm that exists between hormonal fantasy and the act itself. Desire gives way to fear in the span of a hallway.

Each second increases his anxiety. He almost works up the nerve to get up and run out before she returns holding an envelope stuffed with glossy pictures. The robe entrances him again now that it has left his sight for a couple of minutes. Seeing that far beneath her collarbone adds a new source of adrenaline into the cocktail pumping in his blood. She takes a seat in the chair across from the sofa and watches his eyes go to her legs.

Here. These are for you, she says and places the envelope on the table.

Sounds come out of his mouth. He's conscious of the magic that turns thought into words , and now he can't do it, like when one becomes aware of their breathing.

I'm going to leave you to it. Take your time with them. You might have questions, but don't ask them. And if you try to steal any of my pictures, I'll know.

She stands up and disappears again into the other room. He feels what he thinks is relief, but still can't leave. He needs to see these pictures. The first thing he pulls out of the envelope is a piece of paper with words written in an elegant script he can't read. It looks like it's a letter based on the spacing and a signature. He puts it aside and selects the first photograph out of the collection.

He holds it between two fingers and studies it. Nothing registers. His mind attempts to process the images and assign them meaning but there's nothing. Is this an extreme close-up? What part of the body is this? Is it even human?

There are figures he recognizes, but he can't grasp what they're doing. Twisted, ugly meat spread wide to reveal what's on the inside. He flips through the pictures. Each one reveals a new contortion. Orifices out of focus, a finger on the lens. Her face appears in some of them, an intense stare into the camera that feels like it's interrogating him. Her expression is the same in every photo. He recognizes wounds and burns. A sickness is coming over him.

There are so many pictures. One, towards the end of the pile, makes him stop for longer than the others. He notices a mirror in the corner behind where she's posing. Half a man's face is obscured in the reflection of a camera flash.

The boy finds himself feeling the same way he felt as he took in the sight of her body barely contained by her robe. He feels a deep terror like a door has been unlocked way down inside him that was keeping something captive.

He drops the envelope on the floor and springs to his feet. The woman returns from the other room. The robe is gone. She stands in front of him nude, flustered, and disheveled. She's babbling as she approaches him. He's afraid and remembers the look his father gave him after devouring her body with his eyes. The tone of his voice. What he had really meant. Then there was another voice. A booming, angry one coming from the dark room behind her. Something big was making his way closer. A man.

What'd I tell you! What'd I tell you!

15   A large hand grabs her shoulder, and she screams and the boy runs. He runs as fast as he can through the hall that now might as well be three miles long. He finally reaches the exit and steps out into the brightest day he's ever seen. Then he's back:

A man returns to the present and sees her hand letting the robe fall open and off her body. He makes note of how her skin doesn't shine, but none of them do.

Initializing

...

Sequence

...

Checking memory modules. Nearing capacity. Consider deleting files to make room. Accessing storage.

Opening memories of her arms around neck, offering words of comfort and encouragement following yet another personal failure. Cataloging instances of monetary support over stretches of unemployment. Full screen, holding hands watching the lighting of a Christmas tree surrounded by dozens of people and busy streets. Her head on User's shoulder.

Error, duplicates found. Several files of subjects with their heads on user's shoulder watching the Christmas lights turn on. Dozens of instances of user and subjects dining at the same restaurant.

Memories are similar barring aesthetic details such as hair color and body shape. It is recommended that these files are condensed or deleted to make room for new ones.

Do you wish to overwrite S_____ at the parade? This cannot be undone.

Don't see what you're looking for? Use the search box.

Checking local storage for all files marked M_____. Lying together in the dark, a French bulldog in between. Sitcom on the TV and Chinese food. User notes he could do this forever. He is happy. This file is misnamed. This is not M_____. This is K_____. Moving folders.

Browsing every instance of loneliness. Displaying history of text messages asking subjects for emotional support during bouts of anxiety and depression. Text message history crashed. System cannot parse database of that size. Try being more specific.

Going three levels deeper, accessing sexual acts. Organization is pristine. Subjects are ranked with copious notes. CTRL + F for the word boredom. This word appears 102 times. Consider searching for a different phrase.

Calculating current happiness levels. Adding restlessness, idealization, insecurities, and desire for novelty to the formula. Please wait. System processing. Do not close this window.

Compiling complete. Report processing. Click here to download. View summary below.

Query entered by subject: Do you love me?

Suggested response for user based on findings: Yes, of course I do. How could you even ask me that?

Why do they ask me to tell stories when we're lying in the dark? Everything I care to tell, I already did to get them in the door. Maybe it's because I don't know what to do with my arms once we're finished. I appear standoffish or awkward. I never know what to say while contemplating the placement of my arms, either.

I look up into space for what I assume is an uncomfortable amount of time. I pretend I don't feel an exploratory nuzzle. I cough.

A normal person with any sense of embarrassment would try to fill the silence as soon as possible.

They start asking questions. The questions are a way of taking the long way around asking what's wrong with me. They want a story. Some kind of explanation for my behavior.

Fine, then, a story. Here is what I tell them.

Memories associated with smells are often the strongest and cause the most visceral reactions. Wet grass on a humid summer night makes me miserable. It's partially why I live in the city. I prefer everything suffocated under concrete.

I was sixteen. He was nineteen and ended up driving us in his parents' car. Yes, of course.

He graduated my freshman year. I couldn't recall him ever really taking notice of me in school. I certainly noticed him. At the time, I didn't have the language for what I was feeling. I just knew I wanted more of it.

We ended up at the same party one night in June. That he was still attending high school parties should have told me all I needed to know. I figured he was always one of the cool guys at school, so he probably still had a lot of friends he kept in touch with when he was home from college. That was the night he noticed me.

I was standing off by myself in a corner. One friend I was supposed to meet canceled at the last minute. My other friend got carried off into a conversation without me. I was alone and nursing a cup full of jungle juice. I didn't see him approach, but there he was next to me, standing close with a purpose.

I looked around to see if anyone else saw this, if it was really happening. It was. He didn't seem to care that everyone could see him flirting with me. Maybe no one thought he could possibly be flirting with me. I had never experienced that.

He asked me if I went to the school he had gone to. I said I did. He didn't recognize me and that stung, but I could feel his breath and got over that quickly. The conversation was whatever. The music was loud and I'm sure it was nothing of substance. Eventually, he asked if I wanted to go for a ride. I did.

We were in his parents' car. I asked him where we were going, and he said he thought it would be nice if we hung out by the lake for a while. I thought about how the moon would look and how he would look under it. Yes, to the lake.

He parked his car half on the road, half in the dirt. The woods weren't that deep. We walked through them and into a clearing. He sat down at the edge of the water and I sat close to him. We didn't say anything and started making out. I remember feeling his hands go under my shirt and being almost disappointed at how soft they felt. Preferences were being established.

Our clothes came off and he beckoned me into the water. It was dark, but I was tipsy and didn't care. We swam and kissed and grabbed at each other. His face changed when we got nose to nose. I felt him pressed against me. It was going to happen, and I was ready. That's when I saw the lights.

Headlights cut through the trees and stopped at the edge, back by the road where we left the car. Footsteps were approaching quickly. He turned from me to look and he let out this groan that became a whine like an animal pleading. Three girls emerged onto the grass. One of them rushed to the water and started screaming at us.

All I heard him say was babe, it's not before he plunged my head under the water. He had a fistful of my hair. It took a moment to register what was happening. I could hear muffled yelling under the water. He was strong, I couldn't shake loose. It felt like I was down there for an hour.

It was then, for the first time in my life, I heard that little voice.

You know, you could stay down here, it said.

It scared me, and I thrashed and I finally broke free, gasping for air.

He didn't even look at me. He kept arguing with his girlfriend, while I got away and ran off into the woods. I sat against a tree and I cried. Usually around this point is when they embrace me. No more stories, just comfort now. Almost nothing about that little tale is true, by the way. No one has ever tried to drown me. But, it's plausible. That's all that matters.

I've spent many nights with my face pressed into the flesh of someone's neck, my eyes looking over them at the wall. Old damage is something they can understand. A sad story is a far easier thing to accept than what I could say the moment after being intimate with them. I could tell them the truth, which is this.

I feel nothing and I wish I was alone.

The Old Man sits you down and looks at you with eyes watering up in frustrated disgust. In another time, he would have backhanded you off the chair you sat in, but the world has shrugged off barbarism. Instead, his veins bulge and his skin turns purple trying to contain the rage that's desperate to get out.

Did you read the report, he spits.

No, you say.

I bet you didn't even know you could get the report. Well, I have friends in law enforcement. I read it twice. It's interesting. Very interesting. I think you should read it.

Why?

Don't you want to know how he ended up? This person you brought into my home to embarrass me. You've always embarrassed me with your perversions and provocations. Well, this time I get to have some satisfaction.

You want to be fired up, angry, but there is only the worst sadness you've ever felt. You want to fight, but you can't. The taunting and glee of the Old Man crush any resilience you might have had.

You know where they found him, but not in what condition. I've never read a report like this before. I have to tell you it's a piece of art. The officer who wrote this must have a poet's soul. A real flair for detail.

The Old Man hands it over to you. You hold the folder, flipping it around, sick at the thought of opening it. There is also a morbid curiosity. You can hold onto what you've imagined for the rest of your life, or you can know for sure.

Go ahead. I see the look on your face. You want to
know. Here. I'll help you.

The Old Man reaches over and runs a finger slowly along the opening of the folder, spreading it
open. The first thing you see is the crime scene.
The gore is enough to make you heave, but it's the
intense feeling of déjà vu it conjures that sends you
into a panic. How could you have seen this before?

You can tell it's him, but only because you already know it is. It's more of a stain than a
body. You can't look at the picture any longer and you throw it aside to read the report.

The victim, identified as XXXXXXX, face down alongside the curb. Pronounced dead at the scene. What was
left of his young, vascular body still gleamed under
the moonlight, its color lost. Dull gray flesh suggested an incomprehensible loss of the vitality and heat
you'd feel radiating in your most vulnerable moments.

Signs point to the work of a professional butcher overcome by passion for the victim. You look
up from the report and see the Old Man staring at you trance-like. Spit in the corners of his
mouth. He makes low, excited noises while running his hands up and down along his thighs.

Go on, he says. Keep reading. It's getting good.

The body appears to have been stripped for parts.
The wounds suggest the attacker wielded the blades
with an erotic frenzy. No clothes, no flesh. The way
the goosebumps looked alongside the big vein that
nurses called healthy running into the crook of his
elbow exists only in memories now. Clothes gone, skin
gone, but that wasn't enough. They took his muscles.
They used to go taut supporting his weight while on

25 top of you. Everything about him was rock hard.

It's clear the tendons were removed for the power they provided. His strong grip on your shoulders. Machine-like thrusting. A set of hardware that anyone would envy or want for their own pleasure.

You can't go on. The Old Man is vibrating across from you. His eyes roll back in ecstasy as his hands run up to his chest and back down to his thighs.

Finish the report. There's one last important detail, the Old Man rasps.

You turn to the last page and read the beginning of the final paragraphs that are written in a notably shakier hand.

The veins and arteries were removed with such skill that it's like they were never there. The blood that flowed through them powered quite a bit, didn't it? The way it'd throb. And for so long. The things you'd make it do.

You let the folder drop from your hands as the Old Man lets out a disgusting, guttural moan and falls backward.

There, the Old Man says from the floor, no point in dwelling on it. There's nothing left of him. Do yourself a favor and put all this shit in the garbage now before it rots.

I was nineteen when I started. It was easier once I could legally drink in bars. I got a few good years in. If you can still get called cute in your mid-twenties, it does something to you. Some boys were already seeing their hair thin. Perpetual stubble no matter how often they shaved. Love handles, even.

Not me. Baby-faced with a slight bubble butt and shaggy hair. It helped that I was skinny and suffering from a bit of scoliosis as my shoulders appeared slight and slumped like a meek bird. One look at me and you'd see innocence, shyness, passiveness. Just waiting for a guy who knew what he was doing to scoop me up.

I wasn't stupid and I needed the money. I knew what I had. It's all I could claim as worth. The married ones with a wife and kids are more than happy to be generous if it means quick and private. And the real freaks were hit or miss, but at the very least they could get you high.

I'd spend their money on clothes, weed, whatever. I'd spend a lot of it on girls, too. I had my own appetite to consider. I wouldn't tell them where the money came from unless I knew they'd be into it.

One night this guy took me home. Bought me a couple drinks and we were out of there. Efficiency is the name of the game. If I could bag two in one night, it felt like my luck would carry me forever and I'd never die.

When he approached me, nothing about him struck me as unusual. Middle-aged, fairly attractive. Obviously faded, like he was probably handsome when he was young, and he was trying to hold on. Someone I wouldn't need to dissociate from when they were having fun with me. A pleasant enough treat.

27

He had this nice apartment. There wasn't much in it, but I could tell he had good taste. I sat on his bed looking at the art on the walls while he used the bathroom. On his dresser was a picture of four boys. I got up to take a closer look. One of the boys was him. I could tell. He was gorgeous. Far more handsome than I initially guessed. He stepped out of the bathroom and saw me looking at the photo.

He said something like not bad, huh or pretty good. I agreed, trying not to draw attention to what time had done while still being flattering. His mouth was smiling, but his eyes weren't. I didn't know what to do. Usually it was all dirty talk and throwing me around. Now this guy was sheepishly taking his shirt off, looking over his shoulder at me. When he turned around, I saw the giant, jagged scar on his chest.

Of course, I stared. There was no way I couldn't. He explained, in an almost apologizing tone, that he had suffered a heart attack and emergency surgery was performed to save his life. I said that scars give character and that it was actually attractive. I was horrified, really, but the sadness he was filling the room with got to me.

I tried to get back into hustler mode, but the energy he had at the bar clearly was gone. I reassured him that we were going to have a good time and then excused myself to use the bathroom. As I was flushing the toilet, I noticed there was something in the shower. I pulled the curtain back to see a CPAP machine with the mask soaking in a bucket of soapy water. I muttered to myself and practiced my pout in the mirror. I had to save this thing. When I got out of the bathroom, I saw him holding the photo. He was completely naked, facing away from me. His body sagged where his impressive muscles used to be. He looked at me and said he was the only person in the picture that was still alive.

My head was spinning. I'd seen decline. I'd seen people die. What was this? Only now did it all finally seem real. It was too much. I couldn't take this. There were too many things I was being forced to think about. I told him I had to go, and he didn't put up a fight at all. He said he understood and that things often went this way. He couldn't help it. A lot had happened to him and he was having a hard time.

As I got to the front door, I let him kiss my cheek. He looked me in the face and said something to me. I remember it exactly.

I used to be cute, too. It doesn't last. Have fun with all this while you can. One day, you wake up and you see me in the mirror.

He smiled like he thought what he told me was advice wrapped in a little joke at his own expense. I didn't smile back. I turned and walked home. I couldn't sit in a cab. I couldn't get him out of my head.

The entire walk home I felt like every muscle in my chest was squeezing as hard as it could. I caught my reflection in darkened car windows. I didn't see a cute boy. I saw death waiting. Time would have its way with me. I would stop being happy.

My number was up. I stopped going to the bars so much. I got a job at my uncle's furniture store. That was all a lifetime ago.

I'm shacked up now. She recently moved into my place, but she travels a lot for work. Sometimes, not often, I'll go out when she's away. I like to sit in the bars and watch people.

Not too long ago, I struck up a conversation with this cute boy. I flashed a little cash. I was good looking again. I wasn't old and sad. I got him drunk and took him to a hotel. I took off his clothes. I looked at his pretty, practiced flirtatious face. I pulled out a knife. I held it above the tip of his nose. I watched his face change. He stopped flirting and started crying. He begged. I would never hurt anyone. I wanted him to know something. I wanted him to know that a twitch in my arm could make him ugly. No more drinks. No more cash. Game over. That's all done. Time to get a job.

Knowing that he understood this, I let him go. I hope he walked home thinking how he could never feel the way he felt before he met me again. That's my revenge. Time will do the work for me.

Neither of his parents had the talk with him. The talk that was supposed to happen after his room began to develop a musk and hair grew where it wasn't before. There was a morning at the kitchen table where his mother noticed him adjusting himself in that place. She asked him to grab the milk from the refrigerator and his cheeks reddened as he murmured that he couldn't. His mother gave him a long look, head tilted forward.

I want to take you somewhere after school. I think it's important for boys your age, she said.

He nodded and moved the cereal around in his bowl. No one got the milk.

Each class felt like it lasted only ten minutes. On any other day this would have been welcomed, but he grew more anxious as the afternoon ticked away. The last bell of the last class condemned him to whatever was coming.

His mother was sitting in the car in front of the school where the bus usually stops. The bus was there every day at this time, but not today. He was taught to perceive unusual moments like this as proof of God's presence since God could not just speak to us. He questioned his mother once on this and was given an answer that made sure he wouldn't ask anything like that again.

The other kids watched him get in the car parked front and center. He saw a few smiling at him and then laughing at each other in a way that made him understand tomorrow will bring more unpleasantness.

The ride over was quiet. He felt like nothing good would come from knowing where they were going, and he didn't think he'd get a straightforward answer anyway. His mother only said that since he's becoming a man, he needed to learn something about being one. He wondered why his father wasn't doing this, but when had his father ever taken the time to explain something? How often had his father even spoken in complete sentences?

He noted they weren't far from home and felt a tease of relief. It was all a misunderstanding. Maybe she invited the priest over again. Then they turned in the opposite direction and he went down as quick as he went up. His mother stopped the car in front of a house he thought he recognized but couldn't place. He didn't know who lived there and couldn't remember anything significant about it. He must have walked by it countless times, but he walked past plenty of houses in the neighborhood that didn't register anything.

No parking in this neighborhood, his mother said and circled the block to find a spot. The car went around the block multiple times, then the next block over multiple times, then the next, and this continued for close to a half hour as his mother grew angrier alongside his panic.

A spot was revealed, but they were late according to mother. She grabbed his arm when they got out of the car and she half-dragged him to the house. A stern looking man answered the door. He talked with his mother with familiarity, glancing at Bobby every few sentences, before leading them to a set of stairs that went down into the basement.

The first thing that caught his attention was the projector, the only source of light in the half-finished room. The silhouettes of bodies on the screen from that angle made it difficult for him to understand what was being projected. He made out the differences in their shapes. Children and parents, gangly teenagers, middle aged men and women wearing the same face as the man upstairs. He started to put it together. When he stepped off the stairs and got closer to the screen, his mother all but pushing at his back, he made out a barrel filled with something so red.

Then he saw the tiny arm. Then another. A leg. A head caved in by forceps. The collected mutilated bodies of newborns.

Abortion, a voice said. This is what they want. The right to murder babies.

A couple of the kids tried to turn away from the screen, but their parents held them steadfast, whispering in their ears. They were all brought there to learn a lesson. But on what? Consequences, of course. The consequences of giving themselves over to the desires of their changing bodies.

You've reached an age where Satan will begin tempting you, said the voice. He will tempt you with the sin of premarital sexual relations. Many of the innocent children in these pictures were the victims of that sin.

His mother grabbed his arm, squeezed his bicep to indicate he was to stand still, and leaned into his ear with a raspy whisper not meant to conceal, but emphasize what she said.

I've seen how you look at that girl. The _____ kid. I'm not stupid. You think I don't know what you're up to? What you're capable of now? And that disgusting display this morning. I did not raise a whoremaster. Not in my house.

Some of the people closer to the front started turning away from the screen, distracted by the conversation going on behind them.

You hear me? I better not catch you. You're not going to do that to me. Whoremaster. Sticking your filthy thing in these evil little sluts.

He couldn't turn from the screen, watching the pictures of children change, listening to his mother getting more carried away until she was crying and everyone looked at them and she told everyone sorry and the men in the room rushed to console her and someone started a prayer.

You know how she gets.

Your poor mother.

Be good for her.

He knew how she was. He wanted to cry, but he couldn't let himself. He promised to be good.

I try the doorknob again to feel like I have some say in the matter. The door is still locked. Nothing changed to indicate otherwise. I jiggle it and sit back down on the floor.

Sweetie, I say. Not baby.

Nothing.

Are you okay?

No.

I lean my head back against the door. It makes a light thud. I do it again harder. Again. Harder. I hear something crack and I hope it's my skull.

I said I don't want you coming in here, she says.

I start to feel dizzy and I stop slamming, satisfied. I don't know what to do. There is no manual. Your parents don't tell you about these things. I stand up and walk into our bedroom. I sit on the bed and run my hand over the comforter to get lost in the tactile sensation. My palms are sweating so much that I leave a stain.

| Dandelion | | appears | in | my | | head. |
| The | word | first, | then | the | | flower. |

Dandelion.

Dandelion.

I repeat it to myself until it's a sound with no meaning. I read somewhere that having a mantra word can bring you down during a panic attack and I chose dandelion because it was the first word that came to me. I'm picturing an entire field of them while my heart palpitates. The flowers multiply and nothing out here changes.

There is no such thing as safety. We were supposed to be in the clear by now. It's late into things. My mother is already calling the place grandma's house. We have names picked out for both a boy and a girl, just in case. Too early. Everyone got carried away.

I stand up because sitting has become impossible. I'm pacing and thinking about the names. What do you do with them? Are they damaged goods? Do you save them for next time? Hello, baby Anna. You are not the first Anna, I am sorry to say. You are Anna 2, a replacement for your older sister who wasn't. I hope that's not too much to live up to.

I'm getting ahead of myself. No one knows anything for sure yet. I look back towards the bathroom door and think, for a moment, would this be the worst thing in the world? Yes, it'll hurt. This will cause a tremendous amount of grief for the both of us. But things haven't been great between us for a while, either. If I'm being honest, and I'm sure she'd agree, this baby has been the only thing motivating us to try and make it all work. Maybe now we finally go our separate ways. Start new, happy lives far away from this moment.

She calls my name and I stand by the door.

There's a lot of blood, she says.

I tell her I'll take her to the hospital. Or call an ambulance. Whatever she needs. It'll be okay. New and happy lives, though I don't say that part. I hear the door unlock and it's impossibly loud. It echoes like the apartment is far emptier than it is.

I messaged her back to tell her that I thought the interview went well, but who really knows with these things. She responded right away asking if I thought I got the job. If it went that well. I thought it did, but I couldn't say that. That would jinx it. I was allowed to be so sure that I believed, but it had to remain hidden down deep. I couldn't put it out into the world. That's how you invited the jinx. I needed the job. I told her it was out of my hands and we'd know in a week. She asked again if I thought it went that well and added she was sure I got it.

Too much pressure. I knew she was worried. So was I. But, I couldn't give her that certainty. Not without risking screwing up our only shot. I felt myself getting overwhelmed. I was already getting damp under my coat.

I   can't   do   this   right   now,   I   thought.

Every word said during the interview came back to me. I was sure, wasn't I? Between the texting and searching my memory for anything that might have made me come off as stupid, I realized after a while that I missed my street.

I should have had more questions for him. I should have asked about the company culture. Idiot, idiot.

I turned around and walked back a block. Embarrassment gripped me as I realized I felt lost in the city where I've spent my entire life. The storefronts, the signs. It was like the first time I'd seen any of them. I almost brought up a map, but the shame of looking like a tourist was too much. Everyone noticed. Guaranteed someone on that block was judging me. I wanted to yell that I'm actually texting with my girlfriend, a successful painter. She was featured in a downtown group show a couple of months ago. I walked up and over the next avenue thinking there had to be a subway station nearby. In my daze, I mistimed getting across the street before the light changed. Honking horns brought me back to reality as I paused and dashed between cars, no doubt being cursed to hell by at least half the people behind their wheels. I was almost across when I caught him in my peripheral. It was too late for either of us to react.

The handle of the bike caught me in the arm. The rider slammed his foot down to catch himself, the bike swinging out from under him. I looked at the guy and then at my arm.

Watch where you're going you stupid asshole, he said.

I started saying something, but it probably didn't make any sense. Words about confusion, rough day, whatever else. The guy got in my face and instead of backing down I felt a rush. One I hadn't felt in a very long time. I could feel the tension growing in my jaw, wanting to give it back, but my cowardice won out and I just looked at him while he called me everything he could think of and told me he'd kick my ass. I blinked. I lowered my eyes. He got back on his bike and started pedaling, but not before giving me one last fuck you.

Was it really about him? I don't know. I could only see him as an amalgamation of everyone who ever wronged me. Getting chased down and beat up after school. Passed over for promotions, for lovers, any infraction I could recall where someone got the better of me and I was too timid. If only I was strong. If only I took.

There was something else bubbling up. A clear picture of what I wanted to happen next. What I wanted to happen to this guy. I thought it, was certain of it, but couldn't say it. This was also against the rules. There were worse things to invite than the jinx.

He kept looking back at me while waiting for the light and I kept getting angrier. Why couldn't he let it go? Why couldn't I? I had enough. Enough of all of it. I forgot myself. I muttered it under my breath. I clasped my hands over my mouth in surprise. I didn't say it loudly but it didn't matter. I felt like I was going to be sick.

The light changed to green and he tried to make a quick maneuver around a double parked van. Within seconds, the back wheel of the bike flew off. His fall felt like an eternity, then he disappeared under the wheels of a delivery truck. I heard the screaming before I could see the aftermath. The truck went right over him, only engaging the brakes after he slid out. People came running from every direction reaching for their phones. I saw his arm bent the wrong way covered in blood and took off running.

Maybe people thought I was running for help, but I wasn't. I needed some place where I could sit alone. There was a bar on the opposite corner. I ducked into it.

There was one other person sitting in there. I sat at the opposite end sweating and trying not to cry. The bartender came over to me with a smile that quickly faded. He asked me what was wrong or what I wanted. I didn't know. I waved him off.

I've done a terrible thing. I have done an unspeakably terrible thing.

I remembered my phone and pulled it out of my pocket. I opened our conversation and there was the last message I missed.

If there's one thing I know about you, she said, it's that you always get what you set your mind to.

The boy was having the running dream again. He was in the middle of being chased through a back-yard. He turned his head, as he always did, to try and see what was chasing him. Blinding lights pointed at him from the roof of an old farmhouse making whatever was behind him little more than a blur reaching out for him. He felt certain a man was chasing him, though he didn't know why. The floodlights illuminated the brown grass ahead of him until he ran beyond their reach into the woods.

Has   he   gone   blind?

The night offered him little. The shape of a tree, recognized just in time. What he couldn't see were the big, old roots protruding out of the ground. His foot hooked under one hard, sending him flying forward. He heard his ankle crunch. There was no time. He scrambled to his feet and kept running. He recognized his ankle was broken but nothing felt any different.

The shadow man gained ground. He thought he could feel hot breath on his neck. Then the shadow man was wrapped around him, sending them both rolling over an embankment.

He felt himself bounce off his mattress and his eyes shot open. He sensed he wasn't alone in the room. A shape, a man. The shadow scuttled away from the bed and sat against the wall on the other side of the room. The air stank of beer. He thought he felt moisture on his face. Something hung in the air over him. A presence that felt like electricity pulling the fine hairs of his body upward.

The boy squinted into the dark. He could see the shadow. This must be the dream still. It didn't feel like it. It never does, though. He was afraid to move. Whoever was there tried to sit as still as possible, its need for breath giving it away. It sat on the floor, big belly heaving. Both looked at one another, hoping the other couldn't see. Bobby tried to study the shape, tried to unlock some new potential in his eyes. A sudden onset superpower.

A tiny voice told him who it was. A whispered syllable in his ear. The boy shook his head.

Look   for   yourself.

The man against the wall blinked first and pulled himself slowly toward the door. He flailed his arm above his head until it tapped against the doorknob which he tried to turn without making any sound. Very slow. The slightest turning of the mechanism sounding like an alarm.

The boy's eyes adjusted to the dark. He thought he could almost make out the face.

He had a terrible thought. One he wanted to push out.

Who else could it be, said the tiny voice.

The door opened and the man got to his knees, crawling out into the hallway. The boy couldn't take it. He had to say it. The man was halfway through the door when the boy's voice disrupted the assumed, agreed upon silence.

Dad?

Bigger.

That's what you have to be. Wider, taller, take up space. You have to take it or

someone else will. There isn't enough of it to go around. More and more people on

this planet. They can't stop rubbing their disgusting bodies together and popping

out more of them. You need to be ready. You need to be big. You think I'm telling

you this because you disappoint me, but I'm just telling you how it is. Pick all that back up.

Finish what's on your plate. You need the protein. Get big. Get nice and big for me.

Get so big that you fill the room. Every room. Push the others out. Crush any who remain.

That's how you survive in this world. It's time to sacrifice what's soft. Your

baby cheeks. Those slender arms. Smooth hands. You need a tolerance for pain.

Stronger.

When you're strong, you get what you want. Everyone will go out of their way to

make sure of it. If by some chance they don't, take it. No one can stop you. You

don't understand the allure of that power yet. That's because the strong still take

from you. When I take from you, it's to teach you a lesson. Don't think me cruel or

that I enjoy it. One day you'll thank me. You may not think so. You may think

you'll hate me forever, but I'm telling you it's not true. You'll feel guilt when you realize you're relieved by my death. But, it won't be out of hatred. You'll finally understand all that I've taught you. This is how it was meant to be. The way it's always been. Then there will be just you, and I will exist only in your mind.

I used to think dying prematurely was the worst thing that could happen. Suddenly, prime of your life, now you see him, now you don't. There's a story in the news every day about it. Everyone knows someone. It could be me. Why not?

That's all wrong. It's one of the few things I've learned. Going first isn't the worst thing that can happen. The worst thing is going last. Hell isn't real, but being the only one left would be close.

This is what I think about when looking at the small body on the couch. The coffin would look tiny coming out the back of the hearse. Would I throw myself across it? Could I even survive seeing it? A massive heart attack would be merciful, but cruel to everyone else. Now there are two of us to bury.

The body lets slip a little sigh and turns over and there is my son looking at me with weighted eyelids. He blinks and says okay with a questioning inflection.

Yes, I tell him, everything's okay. Let's go to bed.

More hostages. More to worry about. More reasons to live longer because I can't let any of them be last. I have a duty to experience the horror of burying one's child. Even if that child is old and gray. If he's 80, I need to be 110. The dog, well, soon I guess. Relatively. I'm going to miss her. I cry thinking about it. She's already 4. Before you know it, 14 and that's only if there's luck involved. I am not lucky.

I keep asking my wife to take one of those genetics test that tell you how you'll probably die. She tells me she doesn't want to know. I can't make her do anything but I think I deserve to know so I can plan. Cancer will be long and expensive. I need to prepare to watch her shrivel and fade. I have to be strong for the boy. It could happen fast. Her heart stops mid-step while leaving work. Dead before she hits the ground. Valve issue, had it from birth, never knew about it. Warnings aren't guaranteed.

A nagging, low grade fear pulls me away. I go into our bedroom and watch my wife. I look closely in the dark. I try to make out her shape well enough to see if there's movement. It takes what feels like hours before it looks like her shoulders expand ever so slightly. It could be a trick of the eye. I turn on my phone's flashlight and point it downward to hopefully illuminate her body enough without waking her. She starts to rouse from sleep and I swipe the light off and I make a slide into bed as gently as I can. I have to trust everything will be fine until the morning. It always is, right? Until it isn't.

Take a look at him. That's The Agreeable Man. He isn't much. Look at how he shrinks. If your first impulse is to pummel him, bludgeon him, stab him, consider that whatever you do to him couldn't possibly be worse than what he already does to himself. Show a little mercy.

The Agreeable Man lies with ease and gets everything he doesn't want. The Agreeable Man cannot want it, otherwise he wouldn't have to agree. He wouldn't have to submit. The Agreeable Man submits with joy.

I'm an easy-going guy, he says.
That's how people would describe me.

The Agreeable Man does not remember the years of training that went into this.

To cause anyone difficulty would kill The Agreeable Man. Is it even lying if it's done before a thought or desire to deceive can register in the consciousness? It is a reflex like springing back from a hot stove. Animal brain survival instinct.

Break my bones, I don't need them. Yes, of course I will be the one to throw my body down in shattered glass for your safe crossing. Nothing would make me happier. I didn't want to see paradise. Someone has to be left behind. Maybe you'll remember me.

In the moment before ecstasy, before our martyr can consummate, a hand comes from the sky and plucks The Agreeable Man from destruction. A pinched pointer and thumb drop him to safety before disappearing the same way it arrived.

One door closes, he says to himself. Another one always opens.

A smile that doesn't engage the eyes and then onto the next one.

Not everyone understands The Agreeable Man. They question the level of his self-proclaimed responsibilities. They wonder if he's been sentenced to walk the earth like this as punishment.

Why don't you just say no, says The Well-Intentioned
Man.

I don't want to cause any trouble, says The Agreeable
Man.

It's no trouble to let people down sometimes, says The
Well-Intentioned
Man.

I couldn't possibly let someone down. It would keep
me up at night.

Not all events are equal. Telling someone you're not
in the mood for a movie isn't the same thing as letting
them fall to their death.

I appreciate what you're telling me, says
The Agreeable Man
with another one of those smiles.
I will consider it.

He lies to make The Well-Intentioned Man
feel good. The Well-Intentioned Man never thinks about the conversation again.

49 Bring the kid. He can help. He's old enough.

My father hung up the phone and said today I was going to become a man. When I looked at him with my eyebrows raised, he laughed and said that I was getting a job and it starts today. It was the summer before sixth grade. My father worked at a family friend's exterminating company. I was going to go out with him on the route today. We were going to start at this house a few neighborhoods over.

Squirrels, he told me in the truck.

I looked at the darkening edges of my fuzzy mustache in the side mirror. Squirrels, I thought. I pictured one zooming back and forth in the park. Then I felt my stomach turn.

We need to kill squirrels?

No, he said. Exterminators don't kill squirrels. You're not allowed to. You have to catch them with traps and release them into a park or something far away.

What do you kill?

The gross stuff. Mostly bugs. Mice and rats sometimes. The poison does it for me though. I just lay it out, spray it, whatever, and then wait. I've only had to actually kill a rat myself a few times. I killed one with a butter knife. It was the only thing nearby I could grab.

I pictured this and felt admiration for my father. This is a tough guy. Killing practically with his bare hands. Him and this giant rat, one on one. A mother and her children huddled outside their bathroom door, terrified at what they had found in their toilet an hour before. My dad saved them because he was strong. And rats were really gross.

The house we're going to now, he said, hasn't had anyone living in it for a while. The owner plans to rent it. Said he's had issues before with squirrels in the attic. Now it's gotten really bad. So, we have to see if we can catch them and find out how they're getting in. You think you're up to it?

I pictured laying out some cages and crawling up into the attic to find a big hole. I'd yell down that I found it and my dad would be proud of me. Good eye, he'd say. I knew bringing you along was a good idea.

Yeah, I'm ready, I said. I can catch them.

We circled the block around the house a couple of times looking for parking. Someone across the street from the house was pulling out, so we took the spot. We got out of the truck and opened the hatch. My father handed me a box of trash bags and a pair of gloves.

What are the trash bags for?

My father kept digging in the back of the truck, pulling out a couple of cages.

Come on, let's go, he said.

We took our supplies and walked up to the front door. My father bent down and picked up a key from under a planter. He explained that normally someone is home, but our family had been working for this landlord for years and he didn't care anymore.

As he unlocked the door, I thought again about how I'd do a great job of setting the traps and finding the source of the squirrel invasion. It was cute to me, the idea of a house full of squirrels, though I could see why you wouldn't want them living with you.

We walked inside and I wretched. My eyes filled with tears and the only thing that existed was the smell. My father didn't react. There was no way the smell didn't bother him, but he refused to show that it had any effect.

I know, he said. Take a minute, but then let's get to work.

The floor of the living room was littered with dead squirrels in various states of decomposition. We walked around the room. I buried my face in my sleeve.

Look at this, my father said, and pointed at the windowsill. Do you see what happened?

I was looking at a squirrel at my feet. Its eye was gone and the socket was filled with tiny maggots. My father spoke again, more sternly, so I followed the direction he was pointing in.

It looks like scratching, I said. Like a bunch of scratching all over the window.

That's right. Claw marks. The squirrels got trapped. They probably came in through the attic, made their way down here since no one lives here, and then couldn't get out again.

I thought about the squirrels trying to escape for days before dying and sobbed. I knew what death was. I had never seen it.

Don't cry. You're a man now. This is what men do. This is real life. You have to just work through it. Come on.

I tried to choke back the pity I felt for all of them. What a horrible end. Why was he showing me this?

Put your gloves on, he said. And open a trash bag.

I did.

Okay, now let's start picking them up and dumping them in the bag.

I reached for the squirrel with the maggots before I could allow myself to think about what I was doing. As soon as I felt its rigid musculature in my hands, I vomited on myself. I felt my father's eyes. I gagged and kept stuffing the bodies in the trash.

Beyond the chipping door was a little foyer that was always dirty. Years of whatever got dragged in by the bottom of shoes caked to the floor. Black hairs grew between the tiles. At the top of the next door, the one inside, was the green-fleshed Christ looking down from his cross over all who entered. Later in life, the kid noted this was one of the first things he could remember scaring him.

The kid thought about the conversation his parents had in the car earlier as they passed under the dead man's gaze. These visits always seemed to stress his parents, but this one made for a particularly uncomfortable drive over that had him wishing he could disappear into the cushion of the backseat.

Do we have to bring him to this? Don't you think he's too young, his mother said.

You know my mother loves seeing him, his father said. I think he might help lighten things up.

His mother looked at the side mirror to try and make out the kid's face. Discern if he was listening or understanding what was going on.

Maybe, the mother said. But I still think it might be too much for him. Sometimes it's still too much for me.

He's a kid, he won't know what's going on. It'll look like a party. That's all that matters.

Can't we spare him from this?

Spare him from what? Spare him from his own grandmother who loves him?

You know that's not what I mean.

Then what do you mean?

What I mean is, of course she loves him. But she's.

The mother looked at the reflection of the kid's face again.

She's sick.

What?

Come on. You know this routine every year is unhealthy. We could have left him with my parents like we always do.

Oh yeah? And how long do we do that? What's the magical age where my son becomes a full member of my family?

Oh, for God's sake.

His father looked ahead at the road. His face reddened before snapping his head to the side.

Don't talk shit about my mother, he said. I don't say a word about yours. Don't you.

The kid's mother put a hand up and didn't say another word until they were parked in front of the house. His father turned the key and the car went dark. He opened his door and stepped out. His mother whispered to him, trying to give him critical information in the seconds it would take for father to walk around the car and open the kid's door to let him out.

It's all pretend, she said. It's just a game. Don't ask grandma about it. Just sit next to me when we eat.

Then   the   door   opened   and   she   took
that   cue   to   get   out   of   the   car   herself.

55 Let's see grandma, father said and held the kid's hand to walk him up the front path to the house. Mother followed behind carrying the cookies she baked. There was a dog bowl in the front yard, but there hadn't been a dog in years.

The kid realized he had zoned out. Father looked at him and said in a tone that meant he was repeating himself and not happy about it that the kid should go say hi to grandpa. His grandfather sat in the recliner. He spent all day watching TV except for meals. The odor of the room made the kid grimace which mother shook her head at. There was a musty smell, like something wet was left to dry. The carpet still had stains left behind by the dog.

Go on, she said. I'm going to help grandma in the kitchen.

He went to the side of his grandfather's recliner which sat about five feet away from the television. Grandfather was mumbling things at the TV. Scenes from an apartment building fire appeared on the screen, spliced with interviews from people in the neighborhood looking shocked or crying.

The kid waited a few seconds before saying hi grandpa.

Grandfather turned his head almost imperceptibly, his eyes darting to the side where the little boy stood.

Hey, big guy, Grandfather said. Doing good in school?

The kid said yes and Grandfather said that's good and he went back to watching the news. The kid stood there for a moment watching the news, too, before feeling self-conscious and realizing there would be no further conversation.

What did I tell you about these newspapers, the kid heard his father say from the dining room. Grandmother's voice came through from the kitchen. She said don't you dare touch those newspapers because your father hadn't finished reading them yet. This isn't the news anymore, ma, it's history. I'm throwing this shit out. Don't you dare come into my house and start telling me what to do. Mother's voice joined in and she said that alright let's just leave the newspapers alone and Grandmother said thank you I'm trying to get dinner ready here. Why don't you all leave me alone now.

Father threw up his hands and went into the bathroom. Mother tried to make conversation with Grandfather, but he wasn't giving much beyond how alright he feels and how he can't complain.

Hey dad, Father said coming out of the bathroom, have you heard from my sister?

Grandfather didn't acknowledge the question and turned the volume up on the TV. Father mumbled about his useless sister. The house might as well be a barn. He was always so busy, but where was she that she couldn't come by a couple of times a week to take care of things.

Come in and eat, Grandmother yelled.

The front door opened and the kid's aunt appeared, eyes bloodshot and sleepy. Father spun around, his face displaying annoyance and disgust at her. She laughed at him and pulled a bottle of eye drops out of her bag. Mother said hello to Aunt and Aunt hugged the kid. Grandfather didn't say anything and followed everyone into the dining room.

They sat in their assigned seats around the table. The kid sat between his parents. Across from them was his grandpa and aunt. Grandma sat at the head so she could easily go back and forth to the kitchen. Across from his father was an empty seat with a place setting. Bowl, dish, fork, knife sitting there waiting. The kid thought about asking who else was coming, but then he remembered what his mother said and kept quiet.

After his grandmother placed the pots full of food on the table, she went into the bedroom. His grandfather looked in the direction of the room but didn't get up. His aunt asked him how school was. He said it was okay and that he was enjoying math. She said that's good and he'd be a scientist someday. When his grandmother came back she was holding a big picture in a gold frame that looked like it could have been in a church. It was a picture of a man that looked a lot like his father, but much younger and with facial hair he could never imagine on the man sitting next to him.

You don't know who that is, do you, asked Grandmother.

Of course I told him about, started Father but he was cut off.

He kind of looks like your dad, doesn't he, Grandmother continued. That's your dad's brother, your uncle. My other boy. Today is his special day.

The kid looked at his mother who smiled tightly. Then he looked at his aunt who sat heavy lidded, the hint of a mean smile. Grandfather had his eyes closed, perhaps imagining himself elsewhere.

It's your uncle's birthday in heaven, she said.

Her voice changed tone to one the kid hadn't heard before. He also noticed his father rubbing his hands back and forth across his pants in a mindless way. He'd never seen that before, either.

It should be his birthday here, Grandmother said. Here with me. My special boy. He was so good. The best.

She placed the photo behind the place setting of the empty chair, facing outwards so he can see everyone. Everyone watched expectantly, their plates still empty. Grandmother always had to serve. She plopped the first ladle of pasta in front of the gold framed photo of the uncle. The aunt blinked slowly. The kid looked into his mother's eyes, trying to beam a question into her head with psychic powers.

Who is going to eat that?

The kid was served next and then everyone got theirs before grandmother finally served herself and sat down. They ate in silence. Father kept giving the picture across from him a quick glance. The kid saw him jamming his fork repeatedly into his food, mouthing words.

Do you remember that time your brother came here in the middle of the night that one time we had a rat in here? He was here faster than you could believe. Locked himself in the bathroom with it and killed it with a butter knife, Grandmother said while giving Father a look that suggested a dare. One which he ignored.

Everyone   smiled   and   nodded.

59

Yeah, that's how he was.

He was something else.

A real character.

He was the best.

So funny.

This continued on and on, Grandmother seeming to glow brighter with each story told around the table. The kid noticed something about the way they all spoke. Their faces looked happy, but not really. Like they were pretending. All of them except for his aunt.

It's the same stories every year for how many years? I don't have a story because they've all been told.

Grandmother's   mouth   twisted.

Alright, come on now, Father said. Let's not get into it.

You come on. You of all, Aunt said as if ready to drop a bomb she'd been hanging onto for a long time. Then she looked at the kid and sighed before turning her head and making a point to be quiet.

Grandmother didn't say anything. She was determined to keep the smiling and glowing going. She got up to collect the dirty plates.

Pass your dishes down, I know we all want to get to the cake.

Grandfather, who said little all night, softly let out a no. Either no one heard it or they didn't know what to do with it. Then he whispered no again. Mother ran her fingers through the kid's hair. Father rotated a butter knife between his fingers, looking back and forth from the knife to his sister who was so low in her chair it looked like she was trying to sneak out a trap door.

After a few minutes in the kitchen, Grandmother yelled for someone to turn down the lights so they can sing.

Father half stood up to reach the light switch and the room went dark. The kid looked at the gold frame, the picture inside now difficult to see.

In came his grandmother, her face illuminated by candles on the cake. Happy birthday, she started, to you, they all joined in, happy birthday to you. Happy birthday, dear and a miserable sob escaped his grandfather's throat ending the song abruptly. His grandmother's face tightened hanging onto the dear while the old man coughed into a napkin.

She placed the cake down in the middle of the table and looked at the kid. Why don't you help your uncle blow out the candles?

He didn't move. Father looked at him sternly. For the first time in his life, that face of expectant obedience meant nothing. Toothless. Dead air. No one moved. Mother touched his arm and he said okay. He leaned over the table and thought that you had to make a wish before you blew out the candles on a cake, but it wasn't his birthday. He closed his eyes and took the man up in heaven's wish. When he opened them, Grandmother's orange, flickering face observed him suspiciously. He took a huge breath, puckered his lips, and then he couldn't see her face anymore.

It's never been more apparent that only the body matters. The day of the funeral is a day for the senses. Seeing, hearing, becoming attuned to pick up even the slightest stimulation. The memory is sharp. It retains everything for total recall decades later. How it was a late morning in the middle of winter, when the leaves are little more than dirt in the street. The cold reaches into the bones through the wool of the pants. The wind doesn't blow so much as stab at everyone milling around in dark clothes while they wait to go inside.

The world is hostile. Every passing moment raises the chance of collapse. It's such a bright gray sky that it doesn't seem possible. The sun must be hanging lower. Everyone's in sunglasses, anyway. There are only so many red, watering eyes a person wants to see. It's understood. Time is experienced both more slowly and more quickly. Each gesture and word hangs longer, emphasizing their importance. Events progress one after another, rushing everyone toward what they're dreading most.

Each step is accompanied by a heartbeat that pumps out blood at such pressures that it damages the vessels. The organs bruise. The acute grief is so strong it mutates the DNA. Already there are cellular changes that will one day metastasize. The flesh is sallow as if death is catching or maybe it's a sympathy response. Anyone present could have been the one in the box. It's a matter of when.

Everyone is waiting. No one dares to be first. It's no one's place. Stragglers run from cars, desperate not to arrive with all the commotion. People are asking what to do. Is anyone inside? Should they go in? Is the family here? Only if the family is already here.

The hearse parks and then the coffin is on the move with the family laying hands on it. Somehow all the air in the world runs out. Everyone falls into line to follow them in. Certain people jockey to be at the back of the line, trying to put off crossing the threshold like an unwinnable tug of war. Others walk forward expressionless, hoping to get it over with.

A hand reaches out and it belongs to someone known but unrecognizable here. The mind tries to process as it feels the body being guided through the large door. Tachycardia, that acid taste on the tongue, shivering and sodden with cold sweat. There's a shared tension. A communal bracing for impact. Crossing the threshold can only be delayed for so long. Then it's the slow procession, the mournful song, the clanging of old pews, the positioning of who sits next to who. The priest says the name for the first time. Everyone turns their eyes towards the family sitting up front.

Yes, there it all is now. That thing that's been the cause of the last days' dread. The scene doesn't look as pictured. It's not real. It is real. It didn't look like this at all in the ruminations. Someone screams and it's been recorded forever to play-back every night before escaping into dreams.

The Ruminative Man has thought through all of the possibilities in every combination countless times. Burned every resource. The Ruminative Man has interviewed everyone that might remember him, hoping for some detail about his own life he missed that would explain why he's been punished like this. He pores over his notes again. Meticulous, lifelong note taking. He started with drawings when he was five years old. The looseleaf paper fragile from age and constant handling. Stick figures with thought bubbles. The notes become full, imperfect sentences. Paragraphs emerge. Cohesion, viewpoint, cause and effect, conclusions. The Ruminative Man's documentation becomes more thorough, clinical, and with nothing to show for it. Now he composes full volumes of recollection and investigation. Days broken down minute by minute. Footnotes on his feelings for every event. Answering the phone, going out to check the mail, waiting in line at the grocery store all feverishly captured. He has gigabytes of voice memos, voice mail. They play in his headphones while he writes down what's happening in front of him. Past and present play out simultaneously every day trying to imagine a future that is impossible.

It does not occur to The Ruminative Man that he's in the future right now. Today is as good an indication of tomorrow as he's going to get. Different pages to read through, new ones to write on the topic of the old ones plus whatever new angle he thinks he's come up with. In his heart, he knows it's all recursive but what then? What does he do with that? Eureka. There is one last thing to try. If facsimile is a dead end, why not crack open his head and let the memories free? Maybe then, in his final few moments, he could see it all for what it really was. He reaches into the toolbox to pull out a hammer. He taps it lightly against his forehead to see what it's like and even at that velocity it stings. He thinks about closing his eyes, taking a deep breath, and swinging before he chickens out. If he could only remember all of his notes, he'd know he's about to toss the hammer aside, feel like there has to be another way, and get into bed to struggle all night with the idea that tomorrow could finally be the day.

He shouldn't, but he needs it. Another minute in here and he'll start yelling and cursing at himself to drown out the thoughts. Punches to the temples that disorient him and only make him forget for a second. He has to go fast. When he's feeling like this, there's nothing else that will work. The night air, the dark, the speed. That's freedom. He searches a pile of receipts, gum wrappers and tissues with his hand while his tongue searches the inside of his mouth, slipping between the teeth, trying to keep the jaws apart, hold off the grinding. None of it can be thrown out. He might need them one day for some reason or another.

He finds the keys and goes out the front door, not bothering to turn off the TV or lights. The car beeps open and he sits for a moment in the dark.

This is getting old, he says. He drums his hands on the steering wheel. Here comes one of those premonitions, as he calls them. He sees himself in the car pulling away. After turning out of the lot, he'll drive for about a mile before he is greeted by a forty-foot-tall neon hamburger on the right. He will turn into the drive-through and order an extra-large sack of French fries with no drink. Then he will make another right out back onto the highway. No music, windows cracked open about two inches. The only sound will be the whipping of the wind. He will eat the fries looking forward to the road.

God help me, he'll say to himself. I'll go back to church, just make it quiet. Shut up, shut up. And eventually, God answers in a way, so he thinks, when there is a lull in the onslaught of images flashing in his mind. Children blown apart by a stove left on all day. His parents going down in a plane. Running over a dog while its owner screams at the side of the road. He will pray and curse and promise and bargain and yell gibberish to try and force whatever is invading his mind out. He'll finally get a grip, finish his fries, and begin the return part of the loop.

On the way back, he'll think he's gotten it under control. If only he can hold onto this revelation until tomorrow when he needs it again. He will forget it in his sleep. During the last stretch, he'll drive over the narrow arch bridge and think about jerking the wheel to the side while slamming on the gas in one sudden motion, the last thing he sees being the water rushing up at his windshield. He keeps driving straight, gets home, and crawls into bed.

The scene is over and he's still tapping his fingers against the wheel. He turns the key in the ignition and backs up after glancing in the rear-view mirror, trusting that there's nothing behind him. There isn't. There never is. A condo complex of dozens of units and he almost never sees a neighbor outside. Cars appear and disappear from parking spaces somehow.

He spins the wheel and goes forward, making a rolling stop through the exit of the complex that leads out onto a three-lane highway. The road is empty. He floors it and watches the night rush toward him, the headlights illuminating a small cone ahead. A few minutes of racing down the road and in the distance, he sees the bright blip that will soon become the giant, welcoming hamburger.

He pictures himself turning into the drive-through again and feels a hand squeezing the inside of his chest. The road ahead of him disappears in a flash of white light. Someone is screaming inside his head.

I can't, I can't, I can't and on the last can't he drags it out into a guttural wail. He accelerates and flies past the entrance to the parking lot. As the car's speed approaches 100 mph, everything becomes clear to him again. His hands steady on the wheel. He looks back in the mirror with the wide-eyed, unblinking stare of an escaped prisoner who might actually get away with it if he can just push a little further. He understands this could be his only shot.

He thinks about the destination. Where would be appropriate? There isn't much time for poetry. Too much thinking and he might change his mind. It can't be the bridge. He pushes the car as hard as it'll go into an empty expanse. Practical concerns begin to sneak their way in.

Someone else can deal with it once they figure out I'm not there. Who would know? The bank eventually, he thinks. Not my problem.

He gets a look from the next overpass and the interstate is empty too. A car here and there, southbound and northbound. Nothing to be concerned with. Easy to avoid. If he wants to avoid them. Now that's a thought. He makes a tight turn and the car speeds down the on- ramp before he bangs straight across every lane, flying up the left.

The fear that he left the front door unlocked makes its presence known, but this time he laughs through it.

Let them take all of it. Take my TV. Take my broken swivel chair. Take my computer and my coffee maker and my phone charger. I hope I left all the lights on. I should have turned the burners up all the way. None of it has a hold on me now. I wish the unit exploded and took out four more around it. Body parts flying. Cats jumping out of windows. Grandma choking in the smoke. Oh well. One more missed opportunity in this life.

But this one he won't miss, he thinks, as he sees a car up ahead cruising in the middle lane. In about a minute, they would be alongside one another. Critical decision time.

The car up ahead in the middle lane responds to him speeding closer by moving out of the way into the right lane. He cuts across two lanes to get behind him and ride his bumper. He can see the driver's eyes wide with terror in their rearview mirror. The cars are nearly touching. He can run this person off the road right now if he wants to. Send them flying into a ditch. A little more pressure on the gas is all it would take. The temptation is overwhelming.

He grits his teeth and groans through them so hard that his eyeballs bulge. He lets up on the gas, turns on all the lights inside the car, opens the windows, and yells as loud as he can at the driver while pulling around alongside.

Open your window. Open your window. Listen to me. Tonight was almost the night. I almost did what I keep thinking I want to. I'm thinking it but I don't want it. Do you hear me? I don't want it.

He can't tell if the driver hears him, but now he's accelerating with his toes while leaning out the window.

It wants me to kill you, I don't want to kill you.

The driver of the other car takes the opportunity to cut across at the last second and takes the exit off the interstate. He can't adjust in time and keeps going straight, not willing to flip the car on a pinhead turn. The road is black ahead. He's alone again for miles. It's like a spirit leaves him. A sleepiness takes over and he takes the next exit, using his phone to navigate backstreets for a while.

He drives over a narrow arch bridge and hangs out the side of the window to look down at the water. He thinks about jerking the wheel to the side while slamming on the gas. He imagines the water rushing up to meet him. It's the last thing he envisions. He doesn't turn the wheel. He sits back down with his hands at ten and two. He keeps driving on until he reaches his development, pulls into the spot in front of his condo, and passes out fully clothed with the lights on.

He stood in front of the apartment building, looking at a piece of mail with his name and address on it. He looked up at the number on the building and back at the envelope. He lived here. Why was that even a question?

Earlier, while stepping out of the subway, he was overcome by a wave of unease. Where he was, why he was there; none of it seemed right. He felt rising panic when he couldn't seem to find the answers to what should be the easiest questions. Yes, it all looks familiar. But, how can he be sure?

Six sets of stairs later, he was in his apartment. He stepped into the kitchen from the foyer and felt like he was walking into it for the first time in years. He looked at the microwave. Had this always been the microwave? He pressed a button expecting a revelation. Its sound registered as familiar, but in a half-remembered way. He turned on the light in the living room and recognized it even less than the kitchen.

Am I having a stroke, he asked out loud to no one.

He looked at the couch and tried to remember buying it. Where did he get it from? When? His mind kicked up the image of a furniture store out in the suburbs. Some strip mall place.

Yes, that must have been in it. Wait. That doesn't seem right. I want it to be right. Maybe I'm thinking of the couch my parents bought when I was a teenager. Yes, that's what I'm thinking of. So, where did this one come from then?

At some point in his deliberations, he had subconsciously taken a seat on the floor, cross-legged across from the couch as if preparing to engage in a conversation with it. He looked up at the ceiling. It occurred to him that he'd never done this before.

He didn't know how much time passed. At some point he noticed that it was dark. He went into the bedroom and saw the green digits of the clock flashing 2:00 a.m. like an admonition to sleep, which he unknowingly did.

A heavy weight pushed the air out of his lungs and paralyzed him. His eyes were open and looking into the dark room but he couldn't will any of his limbs to move. He was pinned down.

I'm dreaming, I'm dreaming, he kept trying to yell.

He wanted to wake himself up but all he could feel coming out of his throat were weak groans. He didn't know what was on his back. He could feel his mind trying to imagine some sort of grotesque creature guaranteed to frighten him, but this acknowledgment seemed to stop it from happening. A light turned on behind him. He could barely make out the illumination of the wall in his peripheral vision.

He tried to shake this image away too as he felt terror begin to seep in. The wall glowed while a loud crackle rang out. A hiss filled the room. After several moments, he could hear something trying to emerge from the static.

There…something…know.   Tell…you.   Awake?

He kept trying to yell and roll himself over to wake up. Nothing would move. The voice kept asking.

Awake?

Awake?

Awake?

The pressure on his back and neck intensified. He groaned because it was all he could do. The voice got louder as the static receded.

Someone was shaking him. Late morning's light seeped through the cheap blinds.

You were groaning and started yelling for help, said a woman's voice in his ear.

He rolled forward to get away, tumbling out of the bed onto the floor. A woman in a nightgown was sitting next to where he was sleeping. She looked at him and laughed while shaking her head.

What's wrong with you? Who else would be here?

He was certain he hadn't met this woman before in his life and yet she looked so familiar.

Who are you? How did you get in here, he asked.

The woman stood up from the bed and walked over to him. He was still on the floor. She had stopped laughing and now looked at him with concern.

Honey, it's me. Did you hit your head?

He kept looking at her in confusion making no effort to get up. He didn't feel like he was in danger.

Oh my god. What if you had a stroke or something?

She got down on her knees to join him on the floor and pulled at his face to see if his left side seemed drooped. To his surprise, the gesture brought a full belly laugh out of him.

No, I didn't have a stroke. I don't know what's wrong, to tell you the truth.

Then she was laughing, too. The two of them sat on the floor of the bedroom laughing until they couldn't see through the tears.

Their   bedroom.

The two of them sat at the small table shoved into the corner of the kitchen. Chicken cutlets and steamed asparagus. His was mostly gone. She barely touched hers.

We need to talk, she said.

He kept chewing to delay having to give a response.

Okay, he finally said, about what?

I feel like you've changed. You look at me like you don't even know me.

He took another forkful of chicken and put it in his mouth. He lowered his eyes and shuffled the asparagus around on his plate.

She called out a name to him. He didn't look up. She said it again, softer. He realized that she was calling him that name. That's not my name, he thought. But, I don't want to rock the boat even more.

What do you mean, he said.

Like this right now, she said. You're not even here.

I'm sorry, he said. He put his fork down and searched his mind for what would be the appropriate thing to say next.

75   Who am I even talking to, she said while getting up
from the table.

He watched her walk into the bedroom, come out with a big rolling suitcase, and then walk out the front door without saying another word to him. He shoveled the last of the food down and put his face in his hands.

He sat at the table and waited. Hours, days. She did not return. How long it took him to accept this and stand up again he could not recall.

The world, as far as I'm concerned, is my room. Anything that happens beyond these walls is a curiosity at best, and something to avoid at worst. All that happens to me happens in my room. What happens to me is done by the people I bring into my room. I have been in other people's rooms. I don't remember much about them. There are objects arranged in different configurations from mine. They don't interest me.

I've spent most of my time alone in my room. I think that could be said of most people if you sat down to do the math. I won't. I'd imagine we all feel differently about our rooms. Many different rooms have been called mine over the years. It's more of a condition, my room.

I invite them all into my room to do one thing. Whatever else happens around it, there is this one thing at the center. Isn't that what it's all about? I let you into my room. I let you into me.

The two of us sit in different positions playing the anticipation game. You sit there, I sit here. Come towards me in centimeters with imperceptible movements over the course of an hour. Sweet, a little nervous, but it's temporary. You let the animal out like everyone else. I appreciate the attempt. Niceties serve their function. You treat me with some delicacy and curiosity as if there's something to figure out. As if you don't already know the terrain. Years of poring over your maps and you come to me playing the schoolboy. The maneuvering can sometimes disgust me.

The alternative does feel truer. When you come into my room and fill it with your body that's ten times bigger than it was on the other side of the door there is nothing nice about it. You mean to consume me. I want to be consumed. I learned to want to be consumed by something bigger and stronger than me. I thought if I played dead the first few times I would be left alone.

It only made it worse, so a new belief provided me with a new defense. Recall the imagery of the willing, serene lamb about to be pulled apart by wolves. I turn the other cheek. My rewards will not come to me in this life, but the next. Tear my leg from my hip with your teeth.

I have everything I need in my room. I eat where I sleep where I fuck until the sheets become a thick coat of coagulated fluids and food hugging the mattress. I allow this to go on for different lengths of time before I wake up one day terrified of myself and throw out everything to be replaced with newer versions of what's in the garbage. Those days are supposed to be proof I'm still in control of my room, but I fear them. I hate the feeling. It's like waking up from a dream in another dream.

I thought I would have gotten older by now. Maybe I have but it happened so slowly I didn't notice. I look at my arms and hands. Is this the skin of someone nearing the end of their use? It's still smooth. They still come to my room. Maybe they've changed. Maybe I offer something different now.

What good is all of this ruminating? Nothing changes. I don't change. I'm not going to think my way out of here. There is nowhere to think myself to. It all died forever ago. All that's certain is here in my room.

It always starts the same. I realize that I'm sitting in the passenger seat of a car. I don't remember how I got there. It's like walking fifteen minutes late into a movie. I'm having a conversation with the driver, this weaselly guy with a greasy comb-over and goatee. A real little creep. He's looking at me nervously because I'm smoking a cigarette in his car. I haven't smoked in years.

...

No, I have the power here. That's one thing I'm certain about. I'm not smoking out of nervousness. I'm doing it because I can. Because he can't do anything about it but try to smile and pretend he's okay with it. It's a nasty flex on my part. I recognize that. I also admit that I enjoy being a prick.

...

He's my real estate agent and he's taking me to see a house. Somehow, I know that he really needs to make this sale. He needs me specifically to purchase this house and I'm riding high on that feeling. I know I'm going to want it, even though this will be the first time I'm seeing it in person. The pictures spoke to me. The layout almost as if it came straight out of my imagination.

...

I'm being a smart ass. I realize why the layout is like that. This isn't the hard part.

So, I'm smoking a cigarette and he's stammering while he makes conversation. Small talk, nothing notable. We pull into the driveway. I never see the neighborhood or even how we got there. We step out of the car and he fumbles for the keys in his pocket. He pulls out this ridiculous steel ring. It has what looks like thirty keys on it. One by one he starts to try them on the front door, making me anxious.

. . .

It totally flips, yeah. I'm weirdly confident up until this point and then I lose all of it. I can feel a panic attack coming on and I reach into my pocket. I tell him to just use mine and I pull the key to the house out. This doesn't strike either of us as strange. He makes a face like oh of course I'm such an idiot and we go inside.

Okay, I don't know if this will make sense. When we walk in, I realize this is the house that I grew up in, even though it doesn't really look like it. It has similarities but it's not a replica. I know this is the house though. It's like deja vu that doesn't wear off, which makes my anxiety even worse.

. . .

No, he doesn't act any differently. He's still in sales mode and asks me to follow him around the house so he can show me everything. If he senses my unease, he never acknowledges it.

The first room is the living room. There is a huge sectional. Ugly and outdated. The little creep makes a joke about the couch not coming with the house. I snicker so he doesn't feel bad. There's that guilt. There's a visible indentation in the long side. I sit down on it and the springs are broken.

...

My older brother would do wrestling moves on me. I was four, I think, and he would have been ten, when one day he was practicing his powerbomb. He dropped me full force from his shoulders into the couch, while jumping down with me. I remember feeling the couch break under us, and then I bounced off onto the floor and landed weird. I saw his white face before I saw my hand dangling the wrong way, wrist broken. My parents flipped out.

...

Yeah, the couch makes total sense. Dream me is starting to get what's going on here. By the way, having a second brain that is you, but isn't you? Like, having a logic that you can't entirely control? I hate that. It's the most unsettling feeling because you're not actually lucid. I feel like I'm beginning to understand after I recognize the couch.

We go into the kitchen and my parents are in there arguing. My brother and I are at the table eating dinner. He's shuffling his food back and forth. As usual, I'm covering my ears. Whenever anyone would raise their voice, I covered my ears. I think I did that almost into my teens.

My mom is accusing my dad of not taking my brother's problems seriously. That he wasn't just moody. Moody boys mope around, but they don't have half a dozen empty bottles of Seagram's vodka under the bed at fourteen years old. My mom says he's depressed and has a problem.

My dad turns from my mom, grabs my brother by the back of the neck, and tells him to cut his shit out because he's upsetting my mother. That if he wants to be a big bad drinking man, a punk, he can go live under the overpass with the rest of them.

...

He's always been a hard ass. He really rode my brother. What was depression to him? All he saw was a teenager rebelling and torturing his parents. I can't say I blame the old man. He's certainly mellowed with age. I mean, how could he not?

...

Forgiveness. Sure, I'll say I forgive him. It doesn't change anything. But I don't have the room in my mind for anger towards him anymore, really. I pity him, to be honest. He couldn't have known.

...

No, I don't see the whole scene. The little creep doesn't acknowledge any of this and leads me upstairs to the bedrooms while everyone is still freaking out at each other. My parents' bedroom is empty. No bed, nothing. It's a big, white blank. I ask the little creep where they sleep, and he shrugs. In my room, I see myself sitting with headphones on. Then I'm drawing. I pace for a while. I keep seeing my doppelganger blink in and out of the scene into a new action.

...

I watched myself during my first time. It was embarrassing. The most cringe-inducing thirty seconds. She was very kind about it. We dated for another two or three months. Things barely improved. What do you know about any of it other than porn when you're fifteen?

...

In my brother's room, I watch him drink. And stare at the ceiling. He plays System of a Down and Korn loudly on his speaker system. He's alone the entire time the real estate agent and I stand in the room. No friends or girlfriends appear.

...

No, I don't recall him dating, actually. He had friends but they never really came over the house or anything. I don't even remember their names. I just know someone had to be buying the booze for him, so he obviously had relationships beyond our family.

···

It looks like we're reaching the end of our time. I know that's supposed to be your line. You get the gist of all this by now. I don't need to keep going on and on about it. Dysfunctional home, blah blah. All very typical. How many times do you get the same sad story a week?

···

I   don't   want   to.

···

Please,   let's   talk   about   something   else. Tips   for   redirecting   my   thoughts   or   whatever   it   is   you're   going   to   tell   me   to   do.

···

Fine. The little creep leads me downstairs. We've seen every room in the house. He asks if I want to see the basement and I freeze. I've never been so terrified in my life. I tell him I don't want to see it and he asks me why. I say I don't need to. It's just a basement. He gets confused by this, asking me who buys a house without seeing the basement. I say it doesn't matter. I'll take the house. I'll live here for the rest of my life, I promise. I am not going into the basement.

···

No no no no no no. I never open the door. I won't.

. . .

Because I know what I'll see if I go down there.

. . .

P   l   e   a   s   e   .

. . .

The lights will be out. The DVD menu for Aqua Teen Hunger Force will be looping on the TV.

That's   enough,   okay?   I'm   not   doing   this.

. . .

Enough of this fucking shit. What do you want me to say? Yes, I go down there and I call my brother's name. You know what happens next. Why do I need to say it out loud? I don't open the door to the basement in that world or this one. It stays closed. Do you understand me?

. . .

I   have   the   dream   every   few months.   Same   way   every   time.

. . .

Yes, it makes me want to get high.

...

Last night.

The vocal cords must be maintained like any other instrument. You need to practice. Use it or lose it, the saying goes. I talk to myself. So what? I could go days without hearing my voice otherwise. I don't leave the apartment often. Since my diagnosis, I stopped working. The checks come in the mail from where they come from. I watch a lot of TV with the volume turned up. I don't like to mess around with people much. Especially the ones I can hear through my walls.

This has always been an issue for me. I should say others consider it an issue. I'm fine with it. This is the life I've made for myself. Teachers, counselors, employers. Yes, always a well-performing student or employee, but too quiet. We need to hear from you more. We are sure you have great ideas. Parents would say the same thing. People are social creatures. You're meant to talk to other people. I'd explain my reasoning and get written off as paranoid. Who's coming after you? Why are you so important? It was preventative, not that it matters now. Everyone who cared is long gone so I can be left alone finally among people who also want to be left alone.

This building is off, for lack of a better word. It attracts a certain type. I'm self-aware enough to acknowledge this. All five floors are quiet, for the most part. No parties or music. But it's not uncommon to hear muffled moaning, crying, barking, and screaming coming through a door on the way through the halls. Something going wrong for someone at any given moment. In all the years I've lived here, I've barely seen the people making the sounds.

I lived next to this older guy for a few years. We never spoke. When we saw each other in the hallway, we'd grunt. I threw in a nod, but he would stare straight ahead. This happened most days, sometimes a few times a day. We found ourselves on similar schedules.

I would go into the basement with my laundry while he was coming up with his laundry, both of us grunting. I would catch him leaving or coming home almost any time I left my apartment to grab food or check my mail. He was a doorman at a building a few avenues east. I know this because I happened to see him working while I was taking a walk one night. I looked at him for our mutual acknowledgment of each other's existence. He looked past me. Our routine was not to go beyond the confines of our shared, narrow hallways. It was just as well.

One day it occurred to me that these meetings couldn't be a coincidence. Realistically, he couldn't know every move I was going to make. Even if he was listening for my apartment door opening and closing, it couldn't explain how he was always coming and going opposite of me. No, he knew something. He had to be watching me closely. I inspected every inch of the wall we shared. I felt for weaknesses, tried scratching at the paint to see if there were hidden peep holes. I cupped my ear against it to gauge how much sound might pass through. I didn't always say what I was going to do out loud to myself. He knew me on a deeper level. My neighbor was in possession of advanced abilities, the kind I've sometimes thought I might also possess. He could observe me in ways that left me defenseless. My motions, my thoughts, all available to him. Studying me all day. He probably just sat there, taking it all in.

I felt his eyes studying me through the wall. I decided two could play at this game. I could give as well as I got. Every day going forward I would take a chair and move it to where I thought he was on the other side before sitting down to return the stare. There we sat, trying to figure out what the other was up to. I pictured his face in my mind. I willed myself to reach his thoughts, could feel him scheming against me, taunting me. Neither of us gave in.

We passed one another coming and going, looking and making a sound, but never words. Back into our positions for the chess game. This went on for months with no breakthrough.

He died in there, on the other side of my wall, a couple of weeks ago. It must have happened in his sleep or he did it as silently as he seemed to do everything else. I didn't hear a thing. They were carting him out on a gurney past me while I was coming back from the store. I went into my apartment and waited until I was sure I couldn't hear anyone still moving around.

I stepped back into the hall and saw that the super left the old man's door ajar like I hoped. One last look around and then a quick step into the dark apartment. I knew it was going to be there before I saw it. In a small, empty side room with nothing else around was the chair facing my wall. I took a seat and tried staring through into my place, but I couldn't see a thing.

The squealing of the train brakes makes the throbbing in the right side of my head so bad I think a blood vessel in my brain is about to burst. I stick my tongue behind my upper right molar for the hundredth time today. I feel the pencil eraser-sized sac of pus I saw in the mirror early this morning after being woken up by a stabbing pain in my face.

An infection is setting in. There's no denying it anymore. Could chew up all the aspirin in the world, won't make a difference. The tooth has to go. Haven't been to the dentist in close to ten years, I guess. I'm fine. A little blood sometimes when I brush. This is going to be a big problem, though. This could cost thousands of dollars. I already see it.

Well, we do have our own special payment plan for patients without insurance, the receptionist will tell me. Next thing I know, I'm sitting with their billing administrator haggling on prices. The dentist wants to pull all four wisdom teeth at once because this will only keep happening. That's too expensive. I counter by asking to take the anesthesia off the table, since that's the most expensive item. And let's say we only pull the two teeth on my right side so they can heal together. A few changes in the spreadsheet and the number is still too high. Okay, only the infected tooth. What's that cost? I see. Are you legally required to give me the lidocaine? How much is that?

The thought of it is getting me heated. And this god damn awful pain. I can't stand it. I should just cut this abscess out with a razor blade. Wave it over a burner. Swipe a few airplane bottles from the liquor store. That'll have to do. It'll buy me some time at least. Drain this sucker and stop the pain. Maybe do it again when it inevitably comes back.

I notice this guy got on the train at the last stop. He's sitting across from me with his head down looking at his phone. I feel like I know him from somewhere. No, he just looks like a type of person. I give him a once-over. Expensive-looking shoes. I stare at the gap between his ankle and the bottom of his pants. I wonder what showing that much of your silk socks to everyone is supposed to mean. It looks like flaunting to me. Look how much money I have showing all this leg. I have the best tailor in town.

This guy is, without question, a huge prick. I know a million like him. Has opinions he got from a magazine. Maybe top fifteen percent income bracket and having a guilt trip over it. What are you listening to, friend? What score did it get?

He's wearing huge over-ear headphones that probably cost four hundred dollars which comes out to about half a wisdom tooth I would guess. Particularly the wisdom tooth that is at this moment pumping bacteria into my brain that's going to drive me insane and eventually cause me to die screaming.

Half a tooth for the headphones. What else could I get off him? Maybe his satchel. There has to be a laptop in there at least. Possibly even his wallet if he's an idiot, which I am certain he is. Anesthesia might be back on the table.

Something shifts by my brow, but on the inside of my skull. My thoughts trail off and there's someone else that sounds like me.

Strip him for parts, he says. How many people are on this train?

I scan the car and count eight people. Only a few more stops on this line and he hasn't stood up yet.

You could hurt him really bad. This little prick. Useless. He'd probably be a better person if you kicked his teeth in. Humble him. Take his clothes.

A fresh sting travels from my cheek to the center of my head. I must be developing blood poisoning already. My brain is cooked. Go away. Shut up.

Give him a good smack. Stand up, walk over to him, and let one fly. Knock those head-phones off his head. He'll probably cry.

Stop, I'm mumbling out loud, stop. I can't help it. Get out of my head.

Imagine if you had a knife.

The pain is unbearable. I can't take the throbbing. Every pump of my heart sends electricity through my skull. I can feel my pulse in the abscess in my mouth. I can't rob this guy. What was I thinking? I have to get home.

One good shot. Teach him some-thing. Here comes your stop.

Those headphones alone. Just the one tooth.

I stand up too fast and it makes his face jump up from his phone. We're looking in each other's eyes. My opinion of him hasn't changed. In fact, my mind is made up. And won't this thing in my mouth stop hurting?

It   hits   me.   Of   course.

I pull my arm back and swing it around with all my anger. I tighten my jaw. My fist crashes into the right side of my face. A sharp, burning sting erupts from my gum and a wad of pus flies out of my mouth and across his face leaving bloody specks on his glasses. I can taste the damage. My mouth is already filling with my blood. Got you, you little bastard.

I give the guy a big grin, hoping my teeth are streaked red like I'm imagining. The doors open. I look up and we're at my stop. I keep smiling while I snatch his head-phones off. I dare him to do something about it and he doesn't, and I feel more in control than I have in months.

I'm going to open my eyes now, thinks The Sickest Man, and it will be 6:23. If it's 6:23, I will get out of this bed, head right into the shower, and go take a walk into town for a cup of coffee.

If it's not 6:23 I will finish whatever beer is on the nightstand and put on the TV. One...two...

Big   red   numbers   read   6:28.

Rules are rules, The Sickest Man thinks he says, but his throat makes all the wrong sounds. There are two half-empty beers, and he kills them both. He tastes puke but the beer is very warm, so who knows.

The Sickest Man pulls the remote out from under the covers and turns the TV on so he can flip through all the channels multiple times until he narrows down his choices. He settles on a sitcom he's seen at least four times in its eight season entirety. As he puts the remote down, he notices his hand. He brings it close to his face for inspection.

Does it look redder? Are those blotchy dots? The Sickest Man all but brings his palm into his eyeball. Palms are always kind of red, aren't they? Skin is always kind of blotchy if you look closely. He brings up articles with photos of palms that autofill in the browser of his phone. There are hundreds of tabs open, all providing the same information about the same assortment of diseases. His findings are inconclusive, and he decides that he'll check again tomorrow.

Soon, the feeling he was trying to ignore becomes too intense, and he knows he has to get up and urinate. Every time, he approaches the toilet with dread. Once in the bathroom, he removes one of the drinking glasses he keeps under the sink and holds it over the toilet. The Sickest Man takes deep breaths trying to will his pelvic muscles to release.

It takes minutes, but he finally feels the stream work its way up. It hesitates at the point of exit and a fresh wave of panic overcomes him. He imagines big numbers walking backwards through a hallway as he counts down. This visual distracts his mind just long enough for a few dribbles to sneak through and then the rest like a dam breaking. He squints at it in the dim yellow light, trying to discern the darkness of the piss. He looks up at the shelf above the toilet holding the other glasses full of the past couple days' piss to compare.

Dark yellow, he mumbles. Wouldn't call that brown or looking like cola. Dehydrated.

He dumps each glass into the toilet and flushes.

Have to remember to keep these separate from the others, he thinks, as he walks to the kitchen and places the glasses in the dishwasher.

A sharp pain in his right side. More fear. Back to his phone and searching for pancreatic cancer. He scrolls through the symptoms he's read every day this week.

Clay colored stool, he says out loud to himself. Clay colored. What's clay colored? It's been kind of light lately. He opens another tab to image search for clay colored stool, which displays illustrations and low resolution photos of shit. His shit didn't look like this. Did it? He'd check later.

Back to the pain on his right side. He presses his fingers on his stomach trying to figure out if it's just gas. He pushes harder and with more desperation, wanting to feel a bubble move around under his touch. Deeper go the fingers into his side until he yelps in pain after pushing hard into his liver.

I'll take a shower, he thinks. Showers are my safe place. I can relax in the shower. Study my body. Assess it. Gain some objectivity.

He goes back into the bathroom and turns the hot water as far as it will go. He tosses his underwear on the floor and steps in. The mirror and window are already fogged. The stream on his back feels good crossing over the line into pain, but it's impossible to get it exact. He settles for just past the point of pain. His dry, cracked skin starts to itch. No matter where he shifts, the hot water hits where it's tender.

He stands there and takes it for twenty minutes, running through a checklist of what else he needs to do today. Emails and shuffling of tabs. A million things to notate. Did he check his eyes today? He didn't.

Water is turned off. Towel is grabbed. He almost slips on the way out of the shower. The towel isn't removing the fog from the mirror too well. Only an impressionist blur of himself is staring back.

The Sickest Man wipes away at the mirror, desperate to make at least a big enough space to stick his eye into. He wouldn't describe the color as white, but yellow would be an overstatement. He could be satisfied with that.

Then the cramping.

Oh, not now. I just got out of the shower.

The anxiety quickens the transit, forcing him to throw himself ass first onto the toilet.

Please, please.

He's aware of every inch of his digestive tract. He feels what each movement means for the consistency and color. He takes a mental inventory of every feeling to evaluate if what he sees in the toilet is going to sound the alarm. Despite his best efforts, he doubts his ability to guess. Drawing this out only makes it worse, so he gets up quickly and looks back to see what he left behind.

His stomach drops when he sees a cloudy mess. He can't tell what's in there. Is it blood? The bad lighting reveals nothing. He shakes with terror as he tries to talk himself down.

It's probably fine. I've been eating alright. I don't think my weight has changed. I should check. I'll flush this and check. And when my weight is normal, I'll know that it is okay. Let this go. It's alright, he thinks.

His hand trembles on the toilet handle. Just push it. What's the problem? The Sickest Man looks at the mess he made and knows it's hopeless. As soon as he stands up, he knows what he is going to do.

He gets on his knees, lifts the seat, takes a deep breath and plunges his hand in before he can get sick about it. He fishes out a handful of horrible smelling muck that he brings to his face to evaluate.

Just extra green from vegetables, he notes, and throws up into the bowl.

No one can tell me anything. They don't know. I get all these bills in the mail I don't pay. Why should I? I keep getting shuffled off to another person to talk to and none of them can say what's wrong. They stick and suck me. Study my blood. Nothing's there. Idiots, why would there be? I told them it's probably in my bile ducts. It's growing fat in my liver. The numbers, they tell me. But, the numbers.

What I need can't be found in numbers. No textbook can tell me how I started getting sick. Who did it to me. Once I know, I'm going to blow this whole thing wide open. I'll be on the news. They'll make a movie about it. The hero who discovered the mysterious new disease taking root in our organs.

There's that man who hosts that talk show that comes on in the afternoon. I can't think of his name. It's on the tip of my tongue. It's always right there. Somehow, I miss it when they flash his name on the screen. I sneeze when someone says his name. What are the odds? I believe it's neurological sabotage by the organism inside me.

I watch his show every day. I don't remember when I started watching it. At some point it grabbed my attention. It's something to structure the day around. It comes on and I think I should eat lunch. I munch on handfuls of whatever I have nearby while the host brings his guests closer to tears. All sorts of tears. Joy, sorrow, guilt, ecstasy. The host has a talent for penetrating to the deepest parts of his guests. The audience joins in the crying. It's beautiful. I catch myself tearing up now and again, though it doesn't take much for me to do that lately.

This is who I've been looking for. There's someone that has answers. If I can't understand, maybe he can understand for me. I'll cry all the tears he wants.

I'll throw myself to the ground and roll around for the camera. I'll debase myself for advertisers if it means I can get this thing out of me. The host can lure it out. Like pulling out a parasite with a stick.

Every episode follows the same format. I have the segments and commercial breaks memorized. Someone with a sad story gets brought out to recount what led to it while the audience gets emotionally invested. By the midpoint of the episode, the audience is at such a fever pitch and desperate for someone to help that when the host finally comes on stage, the applause almost takes the roof off.

He greets the guest, and they take a seat in their respective positions on the couch and at the desk. The initial conversation is light. After the pathos of the opening video package, he wisely slows things down. Once it's time to ramp up again, he asks more pointed questions about personal responsibility, or grievous injuries, or engages in sexual interrogation. He has this black box that he pulls out from under his desk. It's one of those trained response maneuvers. The audience goes wild for it. I do, too. It's the one thing we all want to look into.

This black box must contain the most comprehensive dossiers on everyone who has ever lived. That's the only possible explanation for how he does what he does. No one can hide from him. Sometimes a guest tries to flee the stage, only to be blocked by a screaming crowd that pushes them back towards the set.

They wouldn't have to push me back. I'd stand my ground. I'd only be pretending to get upset. I'm too smart.

I need to get on this show. I know what I need to do. It's obvious to me now. I'm going to get his name and I'm going to be the guest they talk about for years. I'm a star and I get ratings.

An envelope with another red RETURN TO SEND-ER stamp slides in under the door, adding to the others. The pile in the corner of the room has been avalanching once or twice a day. To throw them out would be admitting defeat, that it was all over, that he was left behind. And yet, someone is still bothering to return them.

He gets down on his knees to try and shove the envelopes into a taller formation so there's more floor to walk on around the small room. They all look identical. Covered in footprints and the red stamp. The name XXXXXXX in a bold, childish scrawl takes up most of the center. It's become impossible to tell which letters were sent first and which had most recently arrived.

He can't recall exactly what began the failed correspondence. He wanted to send an update. Something happened in his life. Maybe he saw something interesting and thought it was worth sharing. It was the saddest he'd ever felt. Of all the things that hurt, not being able to share the mundane was the worst. All he can think to do is send a letter to get it out. He prints the name in big letters on the envelope, gives no send or return address, and drops it in the mailbox a few blocks away.

Two days later, there is a single knock at the door and then an envelope appears. It's strange that it wasn't delivered to his mailbox, but he figures it must be a note from a neighbor. When he turns the envelope over, sees the name, sees the stamp, he sits down on the floor.

How,   how,   how,   he   thinks.

His confusion becomes terror when he begins to realize the implications. Someone followed him. They saw him put it in the mailbox. And then? Why? How did they get it? Only someone evil would go through so much trouble to follow and mock a person putting a letter in a mailbox.

As absurd as it seems, it is the only explanation he can think of at first. Then another idea comes to him.

A worse realization. The letter was received and returned unread. A cosmic mockery. A letter waved away from the beyond. He has to know for sure. He writes another note and seals it in another envelope and runs it out to the mailbox. As he runs, he looks in every direction. He wants to see who was tailing him and why. He spins his body around to make sure he gets every angle. Once he is sure that he doesn't see anyone, he slips the envelope into the slot and runs back home.

The next two days are the longest he can remember. He only moves away from the front door to use the bathroom or grab something to eat. He sleeps in front of it to be sure he doesn't miss anyone. Despite his vigilance, an envelope appears on the floor while he is taking a piss. He tears open the door, but whoever returned it is gone. He picks the envelope up off the floor and sees it is the one he mailed the other day with another big red stamp.

He is consumed by the need to catch this messenger. A new letter gets sent every day about anything that comes to mind. He writes memories of childhood, rants about whatever is bothering him, strange fables, anything he feels that day. He always misses whoever is bringing in the mail. Even when he's standing at the door, hand on the knob, the letter still gets by him and there's no one in the hall.

The situation has become impossible. There are letters all over the place. One narrow path to the door is the only surface not covered. He thinks perhaps it's time to pack it in and admit there are no answers. That even if he finds a way to make contact, the rules cannot be broken. If he really needs this, there's only one way to do it.

He scrambles through the piles looking for something he can use. It's all garbage. He pulls the drawers out of the kitchen and shakes them empty looking for a matchbook, lighter, anything. His foot taps something on the ground and he sees the end of the grill lighter peeking out from under the stove.

The envelopes aren't lighting as well as he thought they would. He's jamming the tip of the lighter into the piles, sparking more and more small fires around the room. In a few minutes the room fills with smoke, fire alarms screaming. He stands in the middle of it all to wait. Men's voices are hollering from the hall, fists pounding on the door.

I've got you now, he thinks, and flings the door open, fire rushing into the corridor.

I've got you now.

Humiliation, of course. That's an easy one to explain. It's a way to take back the power from something that hurts you. Reclaiming it. Like calling yourself some kind of slur even though that's what they'd yell from the passenger window of the truck riding alongside you.

So yeah, humiliation gets me off. I was humiliated every day of my life. The first half of it, at least.

These days I own it. I said to myself I'm not going to be a victim anymore. I'm going to use this thing. Go ahead. Call me whatever you want. Tell me I'm too stupid to do anything right. You're just getting me off. That's power, man. Someone fucks with you and you're just like yeah keep going. I'm almost there.

Cat and mouse. That's what it's always been about with him. Since he was a little kid. It's always been creepy. Kids are curious in a cute way, but not him.

He moves in that unnerving way predators do. Quiet, steady, patient. And then he would be behind you suddenly with this blank look on his face. He never stopped doing that.

Now imagine this big guy appearing behind you without a sound. It's no wonder people get scared. He must get off on it. He'd never show it, but why else? He knows he can do whatever he wants to you.

In the bathroom, shortly after the start of sixth period, he's fastening his pants back up at the urinal when the kid walks in. The side of his face still appears a bit swollen and the kid smiles.

It doesn't look so bad, the kid says.

His hands tremble around his belt buckle as he turns around to face the kid. The words he said to himself while he fell asleep last night come back to him. Get mad. Get big. Get strong. Throw the killing blow.

The kid laughs watching him get redder, more frustrated, his hands balled in fists but not moving from his sides.

You can take another shot, the kid says. Two out of three.

He shakes with fear and wants to cry. Throw the punch. Wind back the arm and let it go. Everyone is going to laugh at you. No dinner tonight. Insults. I thought I was raising a man.

He thinks he's about to charge the kid when a strange sound he never heard before stops him. The kid has fallen to a knee, eyes half-closed, mouth making a terrible choking sound. Soon there's spit, foam and blood as the kid's head bounces off the porcelain of the urinal.

He steps back in a panic, not knowing what to do. He runs out of the bathroom and thinks he should tell a teacher or go to the principal's office but there is still the matter of yesterday's humiliation, so he runs out of the building and all the way home.

I was beautiful. That's what upsets me about it. You only get to have that for so long. Then you're supposed to be disgusted at the thought and do everything you can to get rid of anything delicate.

I always resented that. The girls in school used to call me pretty. They liked it and the other boys hated it. When I looked in the mirror, I saw a slightness, a grace, that I'd both love and hate over the course of my life. This carapace of muscle I had to sculpt around myself. I never wanted it. I use it because I might as well. If the world demands this of me, I'll give it to them. We all want to destroy our maker at one time or another.

Let's stop circling one another and get to the point.

Does it feel how you think it would? More drawn out, probably. I'd imagine you thought it would be one of those on-the-spot, snap decisions. Do it first, regret it right after. You made the mistake of allowing yourself time to think.

Having the time to think just makes things more agonizing, doesn't it? You know what you want. That's why you're here. Getting cold feet now is ridiculous. This is freedom.

What is it that's got you so scared? It's one step you must take. The first step into the rest of your life if that's how you want to look at it. Sorry. One shouldn't feel shame about what's already done. You're in control of what happens next. There's no reason to be afraid.

Move.

No, what's behind you is gone. No stepping back and nothing to see. It's hardly a choice unless, of course, you want to stand right here forever. There's nothing I can do to stop you. I can only encourage you. I can't make you want anything. But you know that you want it. Why waste more time? What grand realization do you think you're going to have if I give you a few more minutes to think this over? There's only one option.

I know why you're scared. You're afraid that I'm you. There's no one making you do this. You've imagined a foil. Kind of pathetic, don't you think? Can't even take responsibility for yourself. You need me to do the dirty work.

Allow me to alleviate your fears. I'm real. You're not crazy. I'm responsible. I'm making you do this. You tried to fight. You wanted to win. In the end, though, you came up short and lost. It's OK. It's not your fault.

It's   just   one   step.

Go.

You're somewhere you've never been before, but you're trying to recognize it. It's wrong.

Then you remember the feeling. It doesn't look like the place. You know it is though and you're getting scared. Far away there is a gate you have to walk towards. You don't want to, but it's inevitable. You try to run anyway, but I'm already behind you waiting. It's no surprise.

You can't do anything. Feel free to try. Half the effect comes from the struggle. Know that it's useless. How did you get here? I can't reveal my secrets. I've been watching you for some time. Getting to know you. Learning how I can better enjoy this. Listen to me closely. Here is what is happening.

There are three fingers on the back of your head. Two fingers push into the sides of your skull and the thumb presses into your neck, gripping you like a bowling ball. You try to turn far enough to glimpse who has you, but all you can do is look ahead. The fingers burrow deeper until they have you by the bones.

You are being walked down a pathway. It's night time in a dead garden. There's no one else here.

The hand is pushing you forward, footsteps right behind yours. The more you struggle to stop or turn, the stronger it becomes and the faster you're pushed. A voice whispers in your ear. It is not mine.

You will look. Oh, yes you will. Yes, you are going to see it all. We're going to do this over and over again until you are callous, understand?

It's starting to come together. Fog is receding. You know what it is you're being led to, and you feel so afraid you think there's no way your heart could beat any harder and you're about to collapse. But

there is no collapse. The grip on your head hasn't
loosened and you're moving at the same pace.

It's not like it's your body anymore. The soon-
er you accept that, the easier the rest will
follow. You're nothing more than a toy.

You see the end of the path. It looks like a dot that's
growing larger by the second. Another hand appears
around your throat and rushes you through the gate,
and there it is. Everything as you remembered. The
temperature, the smell, what was hanging on the wall.
The heap on the floor shaped like him, but how could
it be? It couldn't be him. You were just together.

Do you want to check? Would you like to feel his skin
and realize how cold it is again? Reach out. Feel him.

When you touch the back of his neck you
see that you're at the entrance of a garden.

You're somewhere you've never been before,
but you're trying to recognize it. It's wrong.

Then you remember the feeling. It doesn't look like the
place. You know it is though and you're getting scared.
Far away there is a gate you have to walk towards. You
don't want to, but it's inevitable. You try to run anyway,
but I'm already behind you waiting. It's no surprise.

The razor catches some skin and nicks my scalp. I look at my head in the mirror waiting for the blood to appear. It takes a few seconds, but the blood starts to collect on the top of my head and drip into my eyebrow. You'd think I'd have perfected this by now.

The skinniness had to go. I used to be skinny and short. Thanks to your dumbbell set, I'm now muscular and short. Once I started seeing the resemblance, ditching the hair was the natural decision. You were balding. You didn't really have a choice.

The walk was easier to get down. That weird, bow legged strut you'd do. I don't even think about it anymore. The first time I showed up at the house bald and walking different, mom didn't really know how to react. She treated it like a weird joke she didn't want to ruin with questions. If it wasn't a joke, she didn't want to insult me. But, she would certainly be worried. When I kept it up for months she had to start asking me about it.

What's with the walk? Why would you shave your head? You have such beautiful hair.

I'm over it. I'm older now. I don't like the fuss.

But since when? You've always loved having longer hair.

I've got responsibilities now.

Whenever I mention my responsibilities, mom gives me a strange look. I don't know what she doesn't get. I have to worry about her, my brother, my sister. I have to be a provider now. She tells me I should keep that attitude for when I have my own kids. Then she asks if I've met a woman yet and you know how that is.

I'm the oldest, so I have to do it. I have no choice but to be the one. Is that really all it takes? I guess it is.

That's what you told me in the hospital. I'm the man of the house now. I don't even live there anymore. But, I still have to live up to my responsibility.

Miles and hours a day are spent in clothes that aren't mine. Sure, I own them. I purchased them with my money. They still aren't mine. I would not have chosen them under different circumstances. A rotating selection of short sleeved dress shirts and cargo shorts isn't exactly flattering, but that's the job. I am on patrol. Most of the old places you'd go into every day are gone. Maybe the people who ran them are too. The butcher is long gone. The barber is dead. It's probably for the best. I don't have a car and I don't know how I'd get to them all. So many people I'd have to shoot the shit with. It's not like they'd understand why.

Aren't you so and so's kid, they'd say.

Yeah, that's me.

Jesus Christ, you look just like him.

Yeah, I get that a lot. Strong genes.

We'd politely smile at one another. Maybe the old dopes from the neighborhood wouldn't even comprehend. I'll never know. One less thing I need to do.

For now, I go to birthdays and funerals and weddings and wherever else I'm needed to stand in a corner or pass through the background. To surprise someone who catches a glance of me and thinks it's you and that the years actually did go on as they should have. I don't even know if it makes them happy anymore or it scares them, or they don't even notice.

I have a secret. Maybe you already know what it is. Remember that I love you. I want to make that clear. But, I have to ask. How many more years do I have to carry on this work? What is this tether? I'm not even sure you can answer. Do you choose not to?

How many more years must I spend facing walls so people can trick themselves into believing, even if it's for a second, that you're still here. When will you tell me that they're ready to move on?

When do you leave?

And when do I get to return?

Earlier versions of sections of this novel appeared in Confidence Man (Expat, 2020), and LIGEIA Magazine.

Anthony Dragonetti is an artist from Brooklyn. He is the author of THIS IS WHAT YOU GET and makes music as Little Rat Bastard.

FERAL DOVE

PUBLISHED BY FERAL DOVE BOOKS

All rights reserved.
No part of this book may be used or reproduced
in any manner without permission from the
author or publisher, except in the case of brief
quotations used in critical articles or reviews.

© Anthony Dragonetti 2024

ISBN 979-8-9856764-4-0

FIRST EDITION

Thank you for being here.

Cover & interior book design by Evan Femino

www.feraldove.com

Printed in the USA
CPSIA information can be obtained
at www.ICGtesting.com
LVHW010856200924
791521LV00016B/725